Open the Door!

Open the Door!

A VOLUME OF STORIES BY

Osbert Sitwell

Short Story Index Reprint Series

BOOKS FOR LIBRARIES PRESS
FREEPORT, NEW YORK

First Published 1941
Reprinted 1970

INTERNATIONAL STANDARD BOOK NUMBER:
0-8369-3761-9

LIBRARY OF CONGRESS CATALOG CARD NUMBER:
75-142277

PRINTED IN THE UNITED STATES OF AMERICA

Contents

Contents

Death of a God

The chief difficulty under which at the moment of writing this story the creative artist, but especially the novelist, labours is this; that the violent agitation, from end to end, and from top to bottom, of the background against which his figures are placed, renders the movements of these characters meaningless and unimportant. As well try to concentrate upon a game of chess in an earthquake! The act of writing (if you think of it—which fortunately the born writer seldom does) is comparable to the action of the band which played a march as the great ship *Titanic* was sinking. . . . Well, the loss of the *Titanic*, "the luxury liner on her maiden voyage," as the papers of that day loved to describe her, was symbolic of things to come, but not more than the disappearance from this earthly scene of Mr. Snowberry. . . . With him, for many others as well as for me, went the whole of the nineteenth-century panorama, and especially the works of Henry James and George Meredith. Even more than the novelist of convention, Mr. Snowberry belonged to a dying age.

Ever since I could remember, my life—and long before that, the lives of my parents and their neighbours—had been regulated and set in motion every week by Mr. Snowberry. Without him we should have been lost. He was our god, controlling the life of each week. Lacking his aid, the vague, Meredithian life of childhood in a country house would have come to nothing. Dressed in a faded livery of dark suit, bowler hat, heavy gold chain, which divided his little body into two halves, his face adorned with moustache and whiskers, he drove over the moors to us every eighth day from Bakewell to wind the clocks. The chain I have mentioned supported a heavy gold hunter watch: and by this watch, he set the clocks.

These machines were numerous in all the houses he visited. At home there was the stable clock (the weight of which subsequently proved, appropriately enough, to be the seventeenth-century sundial from the old formal garden, removed to make way for a landscape in

4

the mode of Capability Brown on the stairs) the lac-
quered Queen Anne clock with flamboyant flamingoes
blown in gold upon the surface of its case; the Louis
Quatorze *buhl* clock in the Cocked Hat Room; the tall
walnut clock with a silver dial, surrounded by patterns
of fruit, in the Ballroom; the *directoire* clock in the
Boudoir, which played a minuet by Mozart at the end
of every hour; the tortoiseshell clock with a gold figure
of Father Time and his Scythe in the Great Parlour;
and the inlaid and domed clock which my father had
brought back some years before from Sicily. This stood
in the dining-room, and with an extreme display of
individuality, indulged at odd hours in almost any
form of dissonance that it chose. . . . (And all these
instruments of time, perhaps, were still ticking in the
age appropriate to them, controlling on some other
plane of vision the movement of their coeval puppets;
Dutch figures with periwigs and large, feathered hats
were walking hand in hand in a tulip garden to the
ticking of the walnut clock, while, already coming up
the other side of the Revolution, the *Merveilleuses*
were conducting their exaggerated lives to the beating
heart of the little gold clock; while my parents and their
friends, in the bowler hats, tight trousers and coats, the
tailor-made skirts and leg-of-mutton-sleeved coats, of
the 'nineties were still playing croquet to the rhythm
of that little clock in a leather case which my mother

told me had been given to her as a wedding present.) Thus everything we did or said, our every function and thought and dream, was instigated by Mr. Snowberry. We could hardly have eaten without him.

Moreover, the same thing was true of daily life in all the country houses round; that existence which has now so completely disappeared. On Monday he drove, let us say, to Chatsworth—a hard day's work there!—on Tuesday to Hardwick; on Wednesday—I remember it was always Wednesday—to Barlborough and Renishaw; on Thursday to Clumber; on Friday to Welbeck; on Saturday, perhaps, to Wentworth Woodhouse. On Sunday I imagined he must have wound his own clock (but of that I have something to say later). He was the local god of time: albeit sometimes a breakdown in it caused him to be summoned earlier, so that he became the healer of time, as well as its overlord. At his nod innumerable clocks sounded their silver tinkling, or echoing, rhythmic or cracked notes over the little corner where the counties in Derbyshire, Nottinghamshire, Yorkshire and Lincoln meet. Week after week for nearly fifty years this amiable, good little deity had progressed from temple to temple—this prince from palace to palace.

Round Mr. Snowberry then, the whole invisible mechanism of many great estates revolved. The woodsman in the shrill green light of summer mornings,

Death of a God

when the call to action from the ground seemed to sound clear as a hunting-horn on a frosty morning, rose to his chimes. Later, when the sun had risen above the horizon, and its rays glowed among the feathery tree-tops of the avenue, the horses would begin to neigh in the stables, but the grooms did not get up until Mr. Snowberry's clock sounded the correct hour. In the spring, when, after the hard winters of the north, the bulbs could almost be seen growing, whole russet choirs of birds sang uninterruptedly from the earliest dawn, but even they seemed to cease from their carolling when one of Mr. Snowberry's clocks struck the hour. In the brittle, icy winter, when trees as tall as a ship's masts were roped with frost, and every blade of grass became a crackling spire, it was Mr. Snowberry who roused the sullen housemaids from warm slumber.

On the other hand, while Mr. Snowberry made time advance for others, it seemed, equally, to stand still for him. I had grown from childhood to man's estate without being able to observe the slightest change in him—none at all; not by the greying of a hair, nor by any variation or loss of strength in his voice (which so often betrays the ageing of those who do not show it in other ways) had he altered.

What life did the god of time lead at home, I wondered, between these ceremonial visits to great and lesser houses; between the greetings of grooms and footmen; "Good morning, Mr. Snowberry!" "Good morning, John!" "Pony going well, Mr. Snowberry?" "Yes, thank you, John. . . ." "Lovely morning for the time of the year, Mr. Kembley." "Yes, Mr. Snowberry, what we want is three months o' this, and then tak' op." How did he spend the crisp October evenings, or the lazy summer twilight up there on the moor near the site of the Roman camp, so close under the sky, where heather and bilberries supplied the only vegetation? Just as an emperor is always said to live so simply, to lie on a camp bed in preference to a state four-poster, and to prefer a glass of fresh milk and a rusk to meals prepared by a most skilled French chef, so, too, doubtless this Mexican Prince-Priest, this Maya Time-God preferred, when he considered the riches and extent of his kingdom, to live on goat's cheese, and on bilberries which stain the inside of the mouth to the blue-black of a chow's tongue.

As a child his trade fascinated me and I used to wonder what his own clock, by which he set his gold watch, was like; the clock that governed this god, though equally governed by him; the central clock, as it were, of the whole universe? . . . And, finally, I found out, when I went to tea with him and was thus able, on the same Saturday afternoon, to satisfy my curiosity concerning his house. It was a very small house, not a cottage, with mullion windows, and the stone between them quilted with little pink roses. In the porch stood an enormous very clean-looking wooden spade, which showed very distinctly its grain, and which was for shovelling away the snow, so it should not even in the winter prevent him from reaching the various temples so dependent upon him. The sitting-room was full of feathers, feather-flowers and stuffed birds and patchwork cushions. . . . But when he showed me his bedroom, I was dismayed to find that the all-important clock upon which he, and, in consequence, our whole world, depended was an alarm clock, a common machine of base metal, the tintinnabulations of which awoke him every morning . . . I must have shown my surprise and disappointment for he added, "Well, my dear young man, you see I'm alone here now: Mrs. Snowberry and Esther have been dead these last ten years."

Somehow, I had not previously connected him, so highly did he stand in my regard above mortals, with earthly ties, and it was only then that I realized that the monster over which he reigned had dared to devour those dearest to him; so that his own life was an insecure tenure. His seat on the throne shaky in the extreme. But even when I grew up, I still continued to feel that he should be immune from time's laws. . . . It did not surprise me, therefore, that he showed no signs of growing old. And in consequence I was in no way prepared either for his own final disappearance, or that of the system of which he seemed the mainspring.

Right up to that moment the machine was ticking away without a sign of any internal corrosion. There had been changes, of course: one or two mansions had passed to newer and richer owners (Mr. Snowberry disapproved of such usurpers): no grooms now saluted him, but though the chauffeurs were more independent and wished him "Good morning" in colder, less rural and rather condescending voices, nevertheless, the fact that the motor had replaced the horse seemed only to emphasize the beneficent influence of Mr. Snowberry's activities.

The whole world seemed to be working-up, like a magnificent and ingenious clock, to strike, under Mr. Snowberry's governing, its comfortable, full, rich, traditional chimes. . . . Towards the end of June, however, something went wrong. An Austrian Archduke, who had often been entertained in one of Mr. Snowberry's palaces, fell victim to an unknown assailant, shot while driving in an open motor-car through a distant Mohammedan town. . . . I was with my regiment in Wellington Barracks at the time, and my sister wrote to me from my home to tell me how upset Mr. Snowberry had been at this regrettable occurrence. Just as if a person under his protection had been injured, some sense of responsibility seemed to haunt him, she said.

In July I came home for a month or two's leave, and in the peculiarly golden summer of that year, under the old trees or in the cool interior of the darkened rooms, rumours from the outside world drifted in sleepily. It seemed as if the whole earth were waiting, waiting for bells to sound or a clock to strike. . . . And, being of a superstitious turn of mind, I was unhappy when on the first of August (for by then the outside world had already invaded us with clouds of flying, scurrying reports) I counted the lacquer clock on the stairs outside my bedroom strike thirteen at midnight. . . . It had never done this before, so it must have been my reckoning, I supposed, that was at fault. . . . All the same, two veins of uneasiness now ran through the substance of my mind; one concerning Mr. Snowberry, and the other, for the whole world: (and as it happens, I have never in my life, so far, heard a clock strike thirteen again).

I went to London on the night of the 2nd. On the night of the 3rd, I was among those who saw the Lord Mayor's gilded coach roll trundling up the Mall, moving, unless my memory misleads me, along the narrower side-path strewn with peat moss for riders, to Buckingham Palace; a sure sign of the imminence of the catastrophe that was coming. On the 4th war was declared, and in the morning of the same day Mr. Snowberry met with his accident. . . . Pan and Mars had broken loose together and had set out to conquer the newer god, Mr. Snowberry.

In spite of the general progress, himself had never approved of motor-cars, and he was driving his pony-cart in the neighbourhood of Renishaw when this event occurred. I know the place well. The cinder pyramid of a small mine raised an ugly screen against a wide expanse, in which huge chimneys, plumed with smoke, and stout furnaces raised their bulk. Behind the slag-heap crouched an Elizabethan house, lost and desolate, and then came a rustic prospect in which industrialism did not exist. First there was a lane between deep hedges, and, the other side of it, stood a small stone farm, while beyond, an abrupt perspective of stone walls and meadows that leapt and fell at improbable levels, stretched towards the moors and the far horizon.

Mr. Snowberry was coming down this lane. For all that the coal mines were so close, it was a lovely place in summer, the old stone farm, the near meadows with two spoilt donkeys stretching their furry muzzles across loose stone walls in hope of sugar, the pigs grunting from their sties, or hurrying with their clumsy, fairy-story bodies inflated above short, thin legs, across the green grass—the mountain grass, like the green hair of mermaids, of the high places in this district. Bracken grew high along the sides of the lane, making intricate, lacy patterns. The air coming from the moors smelt pure and mossy, and you could hear the trout-stream purling below. The whole of this vista exhaled a primitive, Noah's-ark charm and offered a feeling of comfort; the green meadow and stone wall, pigs and chickens, donkeys and orchards and stone trough, had always been there and, even in spite of changes for the worse elsewhere, would prevail, and with them a certain rough kindliness. It was this impression of comfort and kindliness that made, perhaps, the shock which Mr. Snowberry was to receive, all the worse.

He was driving quietly along when suddenly he saw before him a white billy-goat tethered tight, but wildly running round a post, rearing up in pain and then jumping down again on its four cloven feet; a pure white goat that was like a flame in its proud, white maleness against the dark green of trees and grass. In front of the animal were two girls, fourteen or fifteen, with the flaxen and tow-coloured hair of the countryside, rolling with lewd brutish laughter, and aiming as hard as they could at the most vital parts of the goat's body. Something in the masculinity of the goat maddened them beyond bearing, for they were at that queer stage of adolescence when young girls are no longer themselves, no longer individuals,

13

their consciousness joining that of all young female things, so that they are able, as we see from time to time in cases of haunting by poltergeists, to produce psychic phenomena mysteriously and with an inexplicable ease. They were laughing under the influence of some horrible kind of intoxication or influence— perhaps at other moments they were good children, perhaps they would grow up to be reasonable human beings, but now they were possessed. The god Pan was loose in them, and they were in reality crucifying that which was within themselves.

Mr. Snowberry, a lover of animals, and who was filled with a loving kindness toward all the created world, made no allowance in his mind for this fury. Anger beat up in him at the sight of this cruelty; he pulled up, shouted, and was just going to jump out of the pony-cart to stop them torturing the poor beast, when all at once they saw him and, in their fright, hurled a stone at him, which hit the pony. The pony ran away and Mr. Snowberry was thrown out, and killed instantly. The watch he carried with him stopped at the hour of his death.

Beyond the sea, as here, the primeval, brutish world was breaking out, and it was several days before the little universe of which he was god discovered what had happened to Mr. Snowberry. Everywhere in Elizabethan long galleries, with their stucco figures in green and pink hose, hunting through dark forests, in panelled drawing-rooms, Palladian stables and Adam dining-rooms, the machinery of the clocks ran down and no chimes sounded the hour. It seemed, my sister wrote to me, as if the figures, too, had run down with the beings that regulated their lives. No one now knew what was going on in the world beyond: no one in these houses knew the correct time to take a walk, to eat, or to sleep. Everything was running down. And in that priest's cell high up on the moors, the metal, clacking tongue of the alarm clock, the central clock of the universe as it were, set by Greenwich, itself remained silent and unwound.

*The Man
Who Drove Strindberg Mad*

Sitting in this large old house, in this freezing winter, in this winter of the world, with icicles clustering their stalactites round every old lead pipe, transforming the implements of utility into shapes of glittering fantasy, much as the mind of the poet changes all which he sees, or the magic of time touches the forest in which lies buried the palace of the Sleeping Beauty, transforming every dull material object into something brilliant and crystal-clear, I thought of lands across the grey and swirling waters where every year these processes take place. I thought of the north—but my mind recoiled from the horrors of Finland and

Russia. Sweden, whatever the immediate future may hold in store for it, is still (as I write) itself, and so I thought of the snowy slopes and bare trees of Upsala, so like a Hoxton print in their clear blue and white tinsel precision, and of the life, on skate and sleigh and ski, so suited to its conditions, which prevailed there. . . . Here the snow drifted in long, upward curves towards the tall eighteenth-century windows, and we watched for the thaw: but all the pipes were solid, and even the telephone wires had in some fashion given way to the spite of winter. . . . And now, as I thought of Sweden and Upsala, of Upsala always more than of Stockholm, all the electric bells in the house began to ring without stopping—the frost and snow working on them in some manner unknown to me, I suppose: but I do not understand the ways of machines or of currents, can form no conception of the tricks by which inanimate objects pursue their careers.

For an hour or more the bells continued, and, thinking of Sweden, my mind reverted to Strindberg, the greatest artist Sweden ever produced, and I wondered how he would have treated this incident, from what cocoon of fiery and unbalanced poetry the episode would have emerged? Because, as you, Gentle Reader, will remember, he was ever assailed by the spite of inanimate objects, trying to plague him, trying to drive him mad. In many books, but especially in *The In-*

The Man Who Drove Strindberg Mad

ferno, he tells us of their dull but deadly machinations, the sponge that threw itself into his bath from the wrong and ominous corner, the picture-frame that fell as he passed, and above all the bells, the bell. The front-door bell, especially, was rung at intervals, day by day, and only stopped when he went to answer it and found no human being waiting there . . . above all, the bells; and as I thought of him, pursued by these innumerable inanimate materializations of fate, suddenly I recalled an incident which I had forgotten, and longed to record it. Not only did it in itself appeal to my way of thinking, but, in addition, it carried me to a distant equatorial land where the heat broods all the year over mirror-like lagoons and where, at dusk and dawn, the thousand little winged inhabitants of the jungle open and close their day with such a shriek of pride and possession as can only be imagined by those who have heard it; so loud and victorious a paean that listening to it throbbing through the ground, through ear and throat and limb, one was obliged to doubt its very existence, it was too loud and insistent to *be,* just as the heat was too hot to be genuine.

I suppose it was because I have so great a reverence for Strindberg and understand so well how his mind worked, and why in its particular directions, and because I think, although I usually do not care to admit it, that his theory of life contains more truth than

21

would seem possible to the dull disciples of everyday (indeed this war is the culmination of his theories, the fulfilment of them upon the *world,* instead of upon the *individual*), that this incident occurred to me. But however that may be, when I was seventeen or eighteen and attached to a cavalry regiment, I discovered two stars for myself, the dire radiance of Strindberg—a light, indeed, from another planet—and the middle-class comforting doctrines of that lesser luminary, Samuel Butler. With Strindberg I, too, watched the conspiracies of little objects, the way they precipitate the imaginative into disaster, and it seemed to me then—as it seems to me still—that in his work was a beauty that, also, lay beyond the world of reason. His heroines could live for years in cupboards, then half-way through the play turn into parrots, and yet they lived in their own burning world of unreason, quite as surely as you or I in ours. . . . In any case I have a special and personal feeling for this sad and tortured author; even though I suppose—I do not know—that I have little in common with him, for fun comes easily to me and I was— I hope the reader will excuse my boasting—born with wit in the tips of my fingers as much as on the tip of my tongue. I have a natural vitality, born of centuries of riding and not-thinking (as opposed to not being able to think); a vitality which it has taken two world wars to destroy. . . . But all the same, in spite of my

The Man Who Drove Strindberg Mad

own innate attitude towards life, I reverence Strindberg as a great writer with, for me, a personal illumination.

The rains were coming in San Salvador: the bootblacks kneeled listlessly at their work and the dark-skinned singers were silent. All day long, grey clouds drifted over the top of the palm trees and a hot wind ruffled and scurried their plumes. An emanation of former massacres seemed to invest the city, the fires of the Inquisition seemed still to smoulder just below the ground, and the rain of bullets that, only a few months before, had been responsible for the deaths of ten thousand Communists, shot *à la Russe* in droves of fifty by machine-guns, seemed hardly to have spent themselves in the air. At the windows, relentless parrots clacked their iron tongues like castanets and gave way to bouts of Delphic prophecy in Spanish. Old gentlemen were eating enormous ices in the windows of the clubs and marimbas sounded their haunting, icy music down the lost alleys of the city. . . . The world was waiting—they, for the rains, and I, for a boat—and so I, too, sat in the club, reading the newly arrived European papers and hearing in them the six-weeks-old rumble of impending tragedy. . . . Every day, as it came, seemed to contain a number of siestas, but of such a kind as to be free of peace, invaded by poisonous thoughts; every night brought the glamour of southern nights, their sounds and scents and relaxations; and to these last I added my private gambler's joy.

At ten-thirty every night I would sit, in that tremendous heat, in a large over-illuminated room, helping, for once, the dull spite of inanimate objects or being its victim. I love even the sound of the roulette wheel and often it has seemed to me that some special link connects its spirit temporarily with those of some of its devotees. For hours at a stretch, without a hint of boredom, I could play this game in which only good—or usually bad—fortune exists, where there is no such thing as skill or intellect: only swift action and luck, and an ability to be for an instant in league with the spirit of the inanimate, the blind, the thing without thought—yet as you watch its revolutions, it seems very surely to possess an individuality, to have its own inexplicable preferences.

Sometimes I can win—though even then the quickness and alertness which, in order to gain, must accompany good fortune, soon desert me, rapidly worn down, like every other gambler, by worry, excitement, fatigue and heat: generally, like all gamblers, I lost. Even then, in this climate, I would find it impossible to go to bed. The heat was too great, the excitement too recent. . . . I would stand for a time on the balcony, watching how even the fireflies in their curves were trying to outline the numbers that lie between zero and thirty-six, watch-

24

ing their scintillating implications, trying to gather their meaning. Then, for a moment, forgetting that I had lost all my money, I would return to the table; only to find myself obliged to assume a passive role. Fortunately I had exhausted every shilling that was on me and so I would sit in a sullen sweat and observe the intricate design in numbers woven by the wheel spinning.

Every night the man of whom I am going to tell you came in very late and by himself, with a pile of chips, and played with an enviable—and yet in a sense, it seemed to me, unenviable—good fortune. At first I thought he was English. He was still young-looking, and rather handsome. He was certainly well dressed and dressed with a touch of vanity, but his appearance exhibited a touch of over-sleekness, while his eyes, hard and yet pleading, seemed to belong to some other body than his own. Their blue and rather cruel, if cringing, inconsistency did not seem to match the physique of the athlete, the rhythmic body, the fair hair and fair skin. For the eyes were cold, very cold for all their strange and inconjecturable pleading. He played with courage, conviction and an almost diabolic luck. I had never seen a man who, at certain times, seemed more sure of what was coming. His long, well-shaped fingers —one with a sapphire and platinum ring on it—knew exactly where to place his stakes: never, for a moment, did he show indecision, although his system was founded, so far as I could see, on nothing but a belief in his own good fortune. There was about him, as he played, something immensely attractive and repellent, an air of mystery. He never spoke: but I could see now that he was not English: nor German, I was sure, he was too like an Englishman for that, so he must belong to Denmark or Sweden or Norway. . . . Yet he seemed at home here. He suited, for all his northerliness, the tropics, as a snake suits the burning ground over which it darts. He seemed very much at home, too, without speaking; and to be on good terms with the world, with people and with things; above all with *things*— hence his diabolic fortune at roulette. . . . But there was nothing mysterious about him. I made inquiries, and was told that he was a prosperous Swedish merchant. He possessed an interest in the railways here, and he also exported coffee and spices to Sweden. . . . It was true that he won great sums. He would not bring his wife to the Casino, for people distracted him: and thus, too, he always entered late, when the majority of gamblers had met their destiny, and his icy judgment came fresh to a community of soiled and broken players and of tired, despising croupiers. In this disruptive world he could hold his own. If he lost, he left: if he began to win, he seized with a cold imaginative power upon his good fortune, and left as soon as it began to desert him. . . . But in the phrase of the gamblers there, "the table liked him." He was its favourite. The dull, inanimate creation beamed upon him as upon one of its own.

Then I met him at luncheon in a pavilion under a tree. The vultures alighted ponderously on their observation posts and watched us with the heavy, hooded eyes of armament kings. Occasionally they staggered, as though from sleep, and turned reflective profiles to the sky. In the darkness of the scrub beyond, many other birds yelled out. The clouds, day by day, hour by hour, were drifting down. There were only present my host and hostess—American friends—myself, and the gambler and his wife. After luncheon our hostess, together with that other plain and resonant-voiced woman, left the table and I sat next to him and we talked. He spoke excellent English, but with a typical northern inflexion. I told him with how great an interest I watched his play, and we discussed many things and places; drifting towards Sweden and then to Strindberg. He did not seem to be proud of the greatest poet his country had produced, though he had lived for a long while in the same small town in which Strindberg had lived while he was writing, among other books, *The Inferno*. I told him how deeply I admired the great writer, but he did not seem interested in such a subject, and wanted to talk of other things or, perhaps, not to talk at all. And then presently, as I insisted, as I continued to dwell on Strindberg (for I felt he must know something of him), I noticed for the first time a light, other than that cold light I had observed in the Casino, illumine his eyes; they flickered with the memory, you would have said, of some past joy, became alive, animated in a pleasurable way. Presently he said in his soft, low voice: "As a boy I used to make fun of him. . . . Often I would run into his garden, ring the front-door bell, and then hide until he had opened the door, and had gone away again, finding no one there. . . . And then, ever so many times, I would creep out, dart up the stairs and ring again. . . . And how puzzled he would look! . . . One never has fun like that nowadays; too sophisticated, I suppose." But I was silent, overcome by horror at this being in league with the inanimate in its dull, cold vendetta against a man of genius. . . . "Childish pleasures are the greatest of all," he continued in his mechanical, meaningless, sing-song voice.

Primavera

By his general nature the Italian is both simple and subtle. Vincenzo, though he came from Sicily, was no exception to this generalization. His remarkable good looks, his delightful, tumbling English, spoken with an Italian lisp, accompanied by a smiling and innocent character (innocent in the sense that a young animal is innocent), but with, in contradiction, a certain almost Chinese wiliness over matters of buying and selling, had served him well. In the space of twenty years he had risen from being a waiter with no friends, no money and little education to owning two fine businesses—he dealt in antiques—which necessitated knowledge and judgment, numerous clients and a fair amount of capital.

Open the Door!

He had spent his first year as a waiter in London, and had then taken a job in an hotel in Oxford. During his spare time there, he had attended lectures in order to educate himself, in a cap and gown given him as a tip by an undergraduate who was leaving. Then in about 1908, in that brief glory of Edwardian days, he had returned to work in London, and had lived somewhere near the Crystal Palace (*Il Palazzo di Cristol:* that figure of speech so compelling to all of Italian race who know the rock-crystal cups and jewelled crystal dragons of Benvenuto Cellini and his followers, and who see in the phrase some towering, overwhelming, superlative creation of the same kind).

He had lodged with Miss Miranda Starbottle, the granddaughter of a Sicilian refugee from oppression. Her grandfather had served Garibaldi and had been obliged to seek sanctuary in England with his daughter in the 'forties of the last century (his wife had died on the journey). In those days refugees had glamour, were not the broken, pitiful creatures that they are today, and this girl, who was beautiful, had soon married an Englishman, a merchant, who had fallen passionately in love with her. Materially, it was a better match than she could have hoped for at home. But Miss Starbottle certainly proved a queer offspring of so romantic a marriage. Her mother had died when she was three, and she had never been to Italy, could speak no Italian, and, except in her dark hair and now faded yellow complexion, showed little sign of southern descent. Indeed, she had always appeared somewhat ashamed of even this element of nonconformity to English Victorian standards.

When Vincenzo first met her, her father, too, had long been dead and she must have been about sixty years old, or perhaps more; equally, she might have been seventy. She seemed never to alter, a typical late-Victorian spinster, frozen into whalebone stays and layers of thick clothes covered with meaningless, fussy ornament, with lace and embroidery and filigree, and with a fringe that crept in black, Medusa-like curls over her forehead; a style which she made no attempt to modify or soften. If she went out—which was seldom—she carried on her head a large black creation, crowned with purple and white ostrich feathers, and in her gloved hands, a mauve-silk sunshade with a filigree silver handle. Over her left temple and the upper part of the cheek spread a large birth-mark: but her face, apart from this livid continent, was sallow and lined, for she possessed the Victorian horror of face cream and rouge, of lipstick and "enamel." She still occupied her father's substantial house in Penge, but she had come down in the world, money was scarce, and she now took in a few lodgers—a few, I say, but no doubt as many as the house would hold. Under her vague superintendence and direction two or three servants attended to their wants. She, as a rule, did little herself for them.

All Sicilians, whether nobles, bureaucrats or officials, are related, and Vincenzo, being in some manner a connexion of hers, had been recommended to her care. At first her frigid manner of living—to an Italian so empty and desolate—her severe abstainer's outlook, her horror of wine and good food, of comfort and of warmth, had repelled him: but gradually he had grown to like her and respect her admirable characteristics, her hidden kindness, her shrewdness—except in business matters—and, above all, her reliability. And, perhaps, the Italian sun so strong in his blood and skin and bones, called out some response in her. . . . At any rate she thawed, became his chief confidant and adviser, a very kind and devoted friend, willing in him to forgive various trifling and impulsive faults which in others she would with severity have condemned.

Thus his occasional excesses of various kinds were overlooked. Perhaps she reflected, in a heart now hidden away, that he was a foreigner and knew no better, or perhaps, even, some similar but repressed strain in her own nature made her exult secretly in his southern conduct. While Vincenzo lived in her house, his parents died in Sicily, and the sense of his loneliness gave her a new and motherly affection for him. "Poor boy," she used to repeat to herself, "poor boy!" And, though formerly she had, because of the same taint in herself, despised foreigners, she now encouraged him to bring his Italian friends to see her. Moreover, Vincenzo dramatized and presented her, until, to a whole circle of Italians living in England, "Miss Miranda," as they called her—for their tongues could not form the alien, syllabic music of Miss Starbottle—became for them, like the Crystal Palace, a symbol of England. And though, indeed, they laughed at her, they respected her, revelled, even, in her thoughts and sayings, as being those of an unfailing representative of her nation and period. And no doubt their coming and going made her blossom a little, softened the hard edges of that drying heart.

Meanwhile, Vincenzo had started his antique business in Oxford Street, and was making money.

When he returned to London in 1919, after the war, Vincenzo decided to open a branch establishment in Naples, and to have a flat there as well, for he was longing for Italian life once more. But, though his shop had prospered, owing to the boom in old furniture during the war years, Miss Miranda and her affairs had, on the other hand, very much gone downhill. All her small investments had collapsed, and she could no longer afford to keep on her old servants: yet without them, she was lost. She could not do the housework herself and her general inefficiency aggravated the situation. . . . She must, by now, have been seventy or over (some people said seventy-six), but outwardly she remained just the same, with no diminishing of the settled richness of curled fringe or lace or jewellery. Her large hat sported the same ostrich feathers; no paint or powder disfigured her face and only the birth-mark seemed to have become emphasized in its wrinkled pallor. Just the same; except that she cried a little when she saw Vincenzo, and that he had never seen her cry before.

When he observed the state of the house, he realized what had occurred. Something must be done to help her, and his warm, impetuous nature decided him at once what to do. With her permission, an English friend of his, a lawyer, examined her affairs. It transpired that if she sold her house, she would be left with about eighty or ninety pounds a year upon which to live. In those days the pound was beginning to buy many lire and so in Italy that income would suffice her.

Vincenzo arranged, therefore, that Miss Miranda should dispose of her belongings, and come to live with him in his flat in Naples. In order to overcome her possible objection, he told her that it would aid him financially if she were to pay him a small sum every week and "look after the flat" (though it was plain that, since she could not look after her own house, and could speak no Italian, this aid was problematic). . . . Indeed, she must have been lonely while he was away, have craved his company and that of his friends, because though her character always led her to oppose any plan, even when she secretly wished for it, she soon acquiesced, after a few protestations that she would "only be in the way," and that before long he would want to marry and be rid of her. . . . Previously she had shown little enthusiasm for Italy, but now, at the age of over seventy, she faced the total change of climate and living that awaited her, with complete equanimity.

. . . . .

By the spring of 1920 they were settled in Naples. Their flat, the top storey of an eighteenth-century palace, faced the Castel del Uovo (that fortress, as the Neapolitans say, that grew out of a magic egg placed there by the sorcerer Virgil), against the classic Neapolitan view of sea, island and mountain. Furnished with part of the stock from the shop, the magnificence of its big and lofty rooms, its gilded beds and chairs and painted hangings and later Empire furniture, might have proved somewhat overpowering to one fresh from Penge. Further, though Miss Miranda's self-respect was propped up on a small weekly contribution to Vincenzo for food and rent, she exercised from the beginning only the empty shell of house-keeping prerogatives. A woman, Maria, came in to cook and do the work, and Pancrazio—a relation of Vincenzo's, a boy of sixteen who helped him in the shop—slept in the other spare bedroom and occasionally condescended to help with odd jobs in the house.

Pancrazio was lazy, everyone saw that at once. He was also untrustworthy and a liar: but the sleepy warmth that broods on the ruined Greek temples of Sicily, where flowers grow from stones and snakes lie baking under them, glowed in his eyes, in his smile, in the movements of his limbs, and this birthright brought him with ease many friends, persuading them to condone the execrable qualities of his nature. His voice, his hands, even, had this warm, animal glow that pleaded so eloquently for him. Moreover, in the shop, he was quite useful, a born salesman (people liked to buy things from him) and in the house he was quiet. . . . Something of the old apprentice attitude to life still lingered in Italy, and so Pancrazio—or Pancras, as Miss Miranda uncompromisingly called him—being, as it were, both friend and servant, would always accompany Vincenzo and Miss Miranda on their excursions and picnics.

His duty it was, to unpack and arrange the luncheon and pour out—and help to drink—the wine. . . . Yes, wine; for Naples was helping to thaw Miss Miranda's disposition still further, and already she drank a little wine. And perhaps—for it could not surely be the beginning of vanity?—perhaps the heat of this spring, when summer had for once started in April, was responsible for other changes. At any rate she had modified her clothes. Her hats had ceased being architectural, were now flimsy, quite gay affairs, suited at any rate to the climate, and she must have steeled herself to throw away several petticoats and tight stomachers, with the result that she had become—though no younger—by several degrees more human and less like an African idol, in the process. Even her fringe she had discarded, and Vincenzo had persuaded her to consult a former London friend, a hairdresser, now chief of his trade in Naples, who was enchanted to advise her concerning the best fashion for her to assume. In fact, Vincenzo was obliged to confess to himself that she had come out of her shell nicely, and reflected credit, and not ridicule, as subconsciously he may have feared, on her rescuer, her Perseus.

Nor did she appear to feel homesick or ill at ease in this strange city, though there was nothing for her to do but to sit on the little arboured terrace, dawdle round the flower-pots, fetch the London papers, or occasionally call at English tearooms for a chat. . . . No, she was not bored: for her she was cheerful and jaunty. She loved, particularly, their excursions: for once or twice a week he would run them out to lunch at

Sorrento, La Cava, Castellamare or Pompeii in his little motor.

How much they had all three enjoyed Pompeii! How often and how long they had laughed during the meal! They continued frequently to refer to this with pride (because simple minds seem to consider laughter as a virtue in itself): how much they had laughed! ... They had not been able to have a picnic within the walls, but had been obliged instead to go to a Swiss restaurant, just outside them. This place, created for tourists, might almost have been built by Bulwer Lytton himself, so full of ancient Roman colour was it: but the food proved to be good. They had eaten *lasagne,* had drunk *gragnano*—that purple, sparkling wine of the district, with its faint, sweet taste of sulphur and strong, deep taste of iron—had listened to an over-ripe warbling of "Sole Mio" by a fat Neapolitan determined to resemble Caruso, had heard blind men clawing at mandolines and singing with a horrible false gaiety "Funiculi, Funicula!" and had, further, watched the antics and grimaces of an old man and woman, dressed in exaggerated peasant costumes of a hundred years ago, who had danced the tarantella with a scrawny exaggeration of youth and grace—all for the price of a rather expensive luncheon. They had drunk a lot of wine which had flushed their faces and given fire to their laughter, and Pancrazio had sprung to life: his

words, usually few, had now torrented over one another. He was transformed. All his sleepy grace became
active and vigorous. But Miss Miranda, though she
looked at him often, could not, of course, comprehend
what he said, though she must have understood his
mood. . . . They stayed there, drinking coffee and
strega, until long after the other luncheon guests had
departed on their earnest task of sightseeing.

When at last they entered the dead city, the heat of
the sun, beating down upon them and reverberating
up from the tufa pavements, seemed to bring with it a
life of its own, so that instead of the individual existence of man or beast, brick and stone formed an entity,
lived and quivered. The droves of visitors had passed
on, and the three of them were able to laugh and joke
by themselves, alone, except for the custodians of the
ruins. The animation, derived equally from sea, sky,
air and landscape, of which formerly this extinct plea-
sure-town had been the scene, seemed to inspire them,
so that they laughed on through the streets of broken
houses, feeling no fatigue.

It had been, in fact, an unforgettable day; one of
those few occasions that happen to come flawlessly
right, so Vincenzo thought; a day with an unforgettable quality of both satire and perfection. Even the
phalluses carved on pavements and walls, and always
so carefully indicated by the guides, albeit explained

vaguely away as "fecundity symbols," appeared not to shock Miss Miranda. (Notwithstanding, Vincenzo, with the curiosity of all Italians in these matters, could not help wondering what the old lady made of them and of their frequency in this buried past.) She had seemed positively anxious to enter certain houses, forbidden to her sex by the authorities, in order to examine the erotic paintings therein. But the custodian obliged her to sulk impatiently in the atrium, while he showed her instead articles of feminine vanity, scent-bottles from which the perfume had evaporated two millenniums ago, and pots of rouge cracked and riven by two thousand years of cinders. . . . But soon the others joined her, and they were outside again, laughing and talking, or sat on a roof watching the faintly glowing plume of smoke that blew just above the baked, purple cone of the volcano.

Naples and the long, viridian spring appeared altogether to soften and humanize Miss Miranda. . . . But in the month of May the atmosphere began to change. At that season the country invades this great city with a magic unknown elsewhere. It turns stones and pilasters, pedestals and broken columns to life. Flowering weeds flamed down in festoons from every cornice and every roof. Age-old and fecund, every scrap of ground, even in the centre of the city, is covered with innumerable and diverse flowers; purple and blue and pink and yellow, they grow from the feet and shoulders of statues and under the trampling hooves of bronze horses. The air itself blossoms with an indefinable life and scent, and a peculiar excitement and heightening of human senses pervades the square and street and room—a sense of expectancy. A subtle uneasiness seems to spread circumambient to every object and every person, and as thus day followed day, Miss Miranda appeared, equally, to become increasingly different, increasingly more human; a touch of coquetry, even, started to manifest itself now in the style of her dresses and her hats.

Presently, indeed, Vincenzo thought that he had noticed that she had begun to use a little rouge and powder. But the idea was untenable. It just could not be, knowing her prejudices. . . . Certainly though, it looked as if the birth-mark had begun to fade out beneath a coat of some thick paint. That was different: probably the consciousness of it had long haunted her, and now, in her new independence, she wanted to be rid of it. Then, too, her hair surely had become fairer? . . . He would try and allude to it some time, in a noncommittal, inoffensive way. . . . But before long, there could be no doubt that she *was* using scent—and a good, French scent. Vincenzo was pleased: he felt it a tribute to his powers of civilization.

The whole time that these gradual yet comparatively

sudden changes were in progress, the full Neapolitan spring was entering into the darkened rooms. The sun, reflected from a thousand walls painted pink and scarlet and tawny red, crept through the shutters and played quiveringly upon the objects within. On the terrace outside the heavy foliage of orange and lemon was sprinkled with white stars, gold-dusted, and the heavy, obsessing fragrance swept through the apartments on every puff of warm air. The vine of the arbour, too, had released tight golden coils, like the hair of the Parian Statues of Antinous and Ganymede which still littered the bed of the sea that now, day after day, exhibited a hundred different suffusions of blue and lilac and green and silver. The Greek frieze of mountain and island, that lay above the water on the horizon, every moment adopted in this golden month new aspects, legendary and fantastic in their beauty. Sometimes Capri opposite looked hazy and remote as the Hesperides, sometimes so near that those who gazed at it felt they could clasp its white houses in their hands.

In the flat, the atmosphere thickened, inspissated, became oppressive. It was often too hot to talk, and things unformulated in speech, and almost in thought, lay behind the lips of these three people, as they sat staring at the sea, waiting for its cool evening breath, or moved with a sullen dream-like quality through the ponderously ornate rooms. Their silence masked with an unreasoning irritability, held in it no contentment of mind or body.

Even Vincenzo, with his happy and easy-going disposition, must have shown his feelings. He often longed to be alone, and wished with fervour that Miss Miranda would not smother herself in scent and—there could be no secret about it now—thus daub herself with rouge. She looked, he admitted to himself at this moment, grotesque, with her hair turning golden (alleged to be its natural colour revived by camomile shampoos), and with her old, wrinkled face smeared so badly with paint that the spot of high colour on each cheek flared up in contrast against the dead white powder of the rest. Her birth-mark, shaped like South America, showed, too, through its camouflage. Why, she was like a Goya; exactly like! All she needed was a bridal veil, and a wreath of orange blossom to make her into one of his *Capricios*. She was old enough in all conscience and, as every Italian knows, dignity and reserve belong to old age. This fantastic mask, and these short dresses and short sleeves, accorded but ill with the corrugated, tortoiselike neck! It would cause any man a passing shudder.

By June, everyone agreed that it must be an unusually hot year. . . . Yet Miss Miranda, who had never hitherto set foot abroad, remained unaffected, scarcely seemed to feel it, except that the dark substance she spread in the hollows under and over her eyes, began to run, tingeing the pink and white. But she was never ill for a day, was always there. And Pancrazio, too; silent, furtive, brooding no doubt over some unpleasant secret of adolescence. . . . Well, by the look of him, Vincenzo thought, he would have adventures. But there it was; the boy was probably bad, he admitted, yet in spite of his lies, he liked him for his young and sulky grace.

Toward the end of June, sleep became impossible. All night long the crowds from the slums of the old city sought cool air on the promenade below, laughing, talking, singing. Odd fragments of unconnected song —silly Neapolitan songs—floated in at the wide-open windows until four or five o'clock in the morning. (What could these revellers be doing, Vincenzo wondered?) During the long nights, as he lay there, he began to question whether the flat was not perhaps haunted? Or was it merely that he was so exhausted by the heat and by trying to sleep? . . . Certainly on several occasions he had imagined that he heard sounds and movements and whisperings in the darkness. Stealthy steps crept along the passage, boards creaked, or there was a secretive shutting of a door; shutting was scarcely the right word, it was too muffled and padded and gentle a sound for that. The hushed sibilance of voices, the suppressed and distant echo of a laugh seemed to lie under the noise from outside, and to come from within the large old flat itself. Yet, it may be because he was tired, he did not wish to investigate. Something, though he had little belief in ghosts, held him back. It must be, he told himself, his own imagination. But he did not mention it to the others, did not wish to give them any information, or they might start a scare, and begin talking and talking about it in the heat of the day.

Then one night—it was just before three—he heard something. . . . Unable to bear the mystery any longer, he sprang out of bed and flashed on the light in the passage outside. . . . There, dazzled and blinking, creeping and sidling along from the direction of Miss Miranda's room, was Pancrazio. He wore an old pair of trousers, but was naked above the waist. Even in these strange circumstances, a certain grace and beauty surrounded him, Vincenzo saw, but something was wrong—he could see that too—and shouting "What are you doing there?" Vincenzo seized him, dragged him into his room, shook him until his bones rattled. A silly smile stretched over the boy's face, but he made no effort to struggle or escape. In his hand, Vincenzo found a hundred lire note. *"Ladro!"* he shouted, striking him, "Thief!" But Pancrazio, though he cowered, seemed stupefied. "She gave it to me, Vincenzo," he said. "I am not trying to deceive you. She gave it me.

I have spent the night with her—many nights, *la vecchia putana!* You never told me I was not to. . . . But it was no pleasure to me, so why should she not give me money? . . . But it *is* true, I'll prove it. You can tell for yourself. You know English. She taught me to say these words, though I don't know what they mean." And out of his mouth came, pronounced with extreme care, a repetition of words and phrases of the most obscene and erotic significance. He articulated syllable after syllable, but without emphasis, like a child who has learned a lesson. Word after word blossomed lewdly, evilly from his lips in the surrounding and culminating silence—for at the moment there came no other sound. . . . And the words carried their own conviction of the truth of his story.

True Lovers' Knot

Even when I first knew him—and it must be many years ago—Carey Totnell appeared to be an old man, with the bearded face of Socrates, only in appearance a more elegant philosopher, tinged, in the passage of time, by the epicurean. He seemed to survive as a type, the perfect bachelor of the 'eighties of the last century, suave in manner, cultivated in mind, leading a life both ordered and orderly. He might— except that his mind was more emancipated—have stepped straight out of the first act of one of Pinero's plays, set in Albany; well-read, in a fashion now almost extinct, a lover of the classics, so that he would often read Greek and Latin poetry for his own enjoyment, his choice was governed by a natural taste for all good things, and he showed, too, a great respect for food and wine. I much appreciated his taste and intelligence and culture, his tired wisdom and kindliness: but sometimes I wondered at the garnished emptiness of his existence.

Only once, I think, did I hear him enunciate, in a deliberate, very individual voice which gave point to every word he said, sentiments that sounded as though in some way bound up with his life. And the theory that he had then propounded, fantastic as it seemed that evening, returned to my mind later when I heard of his death.

I had been dining with him—in Albany, of course— and we were talking alone in a corner of his library, while the others played bridge. I was young at the time and he was rallying me on a supposed desire to avoid family responsibilities and ties. "My dear boy," I remember his concluding, "it's no use your ever trying to escape. You are provided with only a few people among whom to play during your life. Some enter at birth, others drift in later. You can hate or love them as the threads that are their lives touch and knot yours, inextricably or loosely, as it may prove; but that doesn't matter: there they will be at every turn in your life, whereas others, whom you may like better, appear only once, for a month or two, and it will be no use your trying ever to see them again. . . . Better at once to accept defeat and try to like those with whom Destiny has thrown you. It saves trouble; for there they'll be, sure enough, at the end! And so it is, too, with places. In normal times—not, of course, during wars or revolutions—only a few scenes are provided as background to the action of your whole life: to these you seem chained throughout your career on earth, and even when death himself arrives for you."

All those who had ever stayed in Miss Pomfret's house, liked to return at least once a week to see her, because it was easy to look in at St. James's Place and they were sure of welcome and amusement. Moreover, she could boast that strange gift, given to so few, of making all her friends, their friends. Originally, I had found my way thither by chance, her lodgings having been recommended by the porter of my club. But I had soon—in company, indeed, with all her guests—taken a great liking to her. She was a personage altogether uncommon, surviving from the age of Shakespeare, audacious and robust as Juliet's nurse, and with a natural gift for original observation and trenchant phrase. By nature Elizabethan, it had been her earthly lot to live through more than half of the Victorian reign, and so she had learned that now people could be shocked, and that a great many of them deserved the sensation.

However, to tow this warm-blooded, vigorously re-acting human being, built on so magnificent a scale, both morally and physically, with her keen, peasant understanding of men and women (rare, because reached entirely through her individual eyes, in an age when the whole population has been taught to read and write), to attempt to tow her, then, and anchor her within the limited space of a short story, is a little like trying to introduce a whale within the confines of a swimming-pool. We will only, therefore, take a single glance at her large frame, its many rotund con-tours encased in black silk, on which were disposed several gold ornaments, at the high black collar round her neck, surmounted by a little white ruff; which im-parted to her smiling and rather creased face the shin-ing geniality of a Franz Hals, so that, most of all, her visitors liked to see her—as sometimes, but not often, they did—holding up a wineglass under the light, drinking to the health of a friend.

One evening, I found, as usual, a good many people in her sitting-room on the ground floor; and among others, Carey. . . . I had not realized before that Miss Pomfret and he were friends. I remember the occasion well, because she gave us a lively description of her new lodger, above, in the best suite. She had taken a great fancy to him—though he was a spiritualist; a faith of which she could not altogether approve—for he sent her enormous bunches of flowers from time to time, and she admired, too, the way in which he had done up his sitting-room, with, as she said, " 'H'indian 'angings' and H'egyptian bronzes on marble pedes-trians," cats, bulls and hawks. "Five thousand years old, some of 'em are," she said confidently. But now came a sound of a bump overhead, followed by intoning: and Miss Pomfret broke off to remark, "That's 'im. Prying to that blooming 'awk, agine, I suppouse."

She liked to stay up talking as late as she could, till two or three in the morning if possible—perhaps be-cause this to her was a symbol of being her own mis-tress at last, with no need to get up early. So, to gratify her propensity in this matter, I stayed behind after the others had gone, and it was there that she told me she had been nurse and personal maid to old Mrs. Totnell, Carey's mother, from about 1882 till her death in 1900, and had known intimately her numerous—there were seven brothers and sisters—offspring. Their father, a famous counsel, had long been dead, and Carey was the eldest son, the cleverest, the pride and despair of his family. . . . I obtained from her, little by little, a picture of my old friend as a young man; a full-length portrait in the pointillist manner, acquired by placing a blob of paint here, a blob there.

In spite of those same responsibilities, about which he liked continually to harangue me, the inhabitant of that elegant, empty shell of to-day had been, it appeared, fierce, wild and untrammelled, a source of anxiety, instead—as now—of quiet comfort to his relatives. And in any particular difficulty that arose—or, more generally, that himself had created—it had been his very sensible habit to consult Miss Pomfret, since she could understand anything, however unglossed, that belonged to human nature, to ask her advice, and to request her to act as intermediary between himself and his family. Moreover, whatever he did, or whatever she may have pretended to the contrary, she was, in reality, fonder of the gay, exquisite, audacious "Mr. Carey" than of all his brothers and sisters, with their better regulated lives—of everyone, indeed, except his mother, to whom she was devoted.

I gathered that by far the greatest imbroglio (one could not say *scandal,* but difficulty is altogether too mild a word for it) in which Carey had been involved, was a tremendous love-affair with an Italian *prima donna* of international fame. For two years he had lived with Forelli in a house in Welbeck Street, and during those few months there had arisen a succession of tempests and hurricanes, born of the hot suns of her native Neapolitan country, and often culminating in episodes of intense strangeness and absurdity.

Always bounded by the conventions of the Italian operatic form, limited to weeping, storming and threats of suicide, even to the pretence of madness, they were followed by scenes excruciatingly sweet, for all that their airs were yet unformulated, but nevertheless peculiarly unsuited to the social life of the English capital, and the quiet of the London clubs. (I mention clubs advisedly because on several occasions Forelli invaded the upholstered seclusion of the Mausoleum in quest of Carey, and had had to be barred from a search of its cloistral apartments by an unspeakably shocked, if comprehending, hall-porter.)

The effect of this upon his relatives can be imagined. They had accused him of bringing scandal on the family, and of neglecting his affairs in the City. Accordingly, Miss Pomfret had often been designated to approach him with suggestions of reform. But, as it happened, Miss Pomfret was, rather surprisingly, a great lover of grand opera; which, together with racing, were the twin lights of her life. Moreover, Forelli had taken a great liking to her, and this flattered such an amateur. . . . Indeed, in only two matters had Miss Pomfret stood against the lovers; she blamed him for causing continual worry to his mother, and she did not want them to marry. ("It wouldn't do.") But in any case, nothing would have persuaded Forelli to marry him, and this had been, in fact—though his relatives were too proud to believe it—the most frequent cause of the quarrels between them.

Open the Door!

Opera has fallen low in man's esteem, and no one now, I am aware, ever falls in love with a *prima donna,* but in those halcyon days of waists and bustles and bonnets, of hansom-cabs and top-hats and frock-coats, when life was serene and unruffled except for the disturbances that you, as an individual, chose to make for your own diversion, nightingales were lovely of feather, as of voice. Into the brief space of their singing lives they crammed whole careers of artistic and amorous experience. When, for an immense fee, paid in gold sovereigns, such a diva consented to sing at a private house, at the mere opening of her lips talk would die away as though the archangel of music himself had entered the room and clapped his wings for silence. And the crowds that applauded her singing would be interested, equally, in the events of her private existence, would be in possession of a great many true, as well as false details, and would discuss them eagerly. Every night elegant, ardent young amateurs waited outside the stage door to see Forelli emerge and drive off with Carey in his private hansom, and nearly every day, too, he could be seen attending her in the Park, or escorting her through a restaurant with something of the pride of a drumming peacock. Bouquets and messages, lyres and harps and wreaths of roses and carnations, arrived for her at all hours. And these trib-

utes helped to charge the atmosphere suitably for scenes
of passion in real life.

In spite of their reasonless and perpetual differences,
in spite of incongruity, in spite of her willingness to
live with, and yet steadfast refusal to marry him, each
had been in reality devoted to the other. Carey was in
love with her voice as much as her person, and for him
she would sing as for no one else. Notwithstanding
frequent ludicrous and painful situations there had
existed in their relationship a quality not only genuine,
but tragic and unforgettable, and this Miss Pomfret had
seen for herself and somehow managed to convey to
me, even after the passing of many years. Here, then,
in the drawing-room of his house in Welbeck Street,
the turmoil of both their lives had spent itself (for,
being a born *prima donna,* she preferred scenes set in
the drawing-room to, as it were, bedroom scenes), and
had loved and quarrelled with a vehemence and ebul-
lition unsuited to this city and its surroundings, had
often parted for ever only to return, dove-like, within
a few hours. Here, with her back to the huge piano
smothered up in a Chinese shawl, with many objects
standing upon it, she had practised her parts, and trilled
her joys and griefs in coloratura.

Miss Pomfret described the room well, could even
remember the identity of some of the silver-framed,

enthusiastically-autographed portraits of tenors with whom Forelli had sung, for she had often been sent there with messages from anxious relatives, or had been summoned by one or other of the lovers themselves. Evidently Carey had furnished it for his mistress with an ostentation born of the recent romances of Ouida and of the influence of Sarah Bernhardt, had filled it with arabesque hangings, with Persian rugs and flowers and palm trees, with bronzes and fine pictures, ancient and modern, and Forelli, for her part, had added operatic trophies, crowns and sheaves of flowers, photographs of elephantine tenors in armour, or with lace collars and hats crowned with flowing feathers. Certainly for him, the place had been charged with vital vibrations such as he was never to give out, or receive, again. The battery, the dynamo of his soul, had been, for those two short years, working at its highest pressure. After that, he became the shell I knew.

Eventually the lovers had quarrelled and really parted for good, much to the satisfaction of all concerned, except themselves. And not long after, Forelli had died in Paris, still in the height of her powers and her celebrity, so that only the echo of that golden voice lingered in the minds of men.

Miss Pomfret told me first of Carey's death. He had been nearly seventy—a good span, I suppose: but somehow, all his qualities, physical and mental, had appeared to be specifically calculated to support him into extreme old age, so that the news came as a shock to his friends. Though, as I perceived, she deeply felt his loss, and his sufferings, yet, reverting again to her Elizabethan character, she could not help manifesting something of Webster's fascinated delight in death. She showed herself determined, in spite—or, perhaps, because—of my affection for him, to spare me no detail of Carey's final distress and dissolution. One could almost hear in her voice, as she talked, the rhythm of the poet's lines:

> Of what is't fools make such vain keeping?
> Sin their conception, their birth weeping,
> Their life a general mist of error,
> Their death a hideous storm of terror.

When he sent for her, she had found him in a typically fashionable nursing-home, made up of several old houses, superficially altered. The lift, she had noticed, was hardly wide enough to hold her, but possessed a curious, long rectangular shape, just able to receive a coffin when it came down.

"Oh yes, he's getting on nicely," the sister had said in a "pleasant" voice cool and clear, "and much more 'comfy' than he would be at home. . . . There's always a nurse with him, even at night, to cheer him up. And he's much less grumpy: quite affable to everyone now."

Carey Totnell lay, propped up on pillows, in a large front room on the first floor; rather dark, and to Miss Pomfret's way of thinking, "too cold-looking," with its sanitary surfaces and enamelling. It contained, too, a litter of pseudo-scientific apparatus, lamps and cylinders and bed-tables, and of spindly fittings in aluminium and steel, the uses of which remain fortunately unknown to the lay mind. "Why, the very bed 'e lay h'in 'ad more the look to me of a dentist's chair than a Christian bed," Miss Pomfret remarked to me. . . . Nevertheless, she had rather liked the room, it had seemed in some way familiar and, in consequence, comfortable and not to be feared.

But she was shocked at the change she saw in the invalid, for he had paid her one of his usual visits, apparently in his normal health, only a few evenings previously. Carey had betrayed from the first, it seems, "that nasty blue look," his voice had come from far away when he spoke, his nails "'ad no life in them," and his hands kept plucking at the sheets; all these symptoms being well-known harbingers of death in the system of divining which she had projected for herself. "You'll never come h'out of 'ere, except a corpse, laid h'out flat in that lift, my man,' h'I said to myself," she added, "but, of course, h'I didn't let 'im see anything. H'I couldn't 'elp crying a little, and jest said,

'Oh, Mr. Carey, dear, to think of seeing you *like this!*' "

The sister had first turned the nurse out of the room, then, after indulging in a miniature power-drive, patting and tugging at the pillows which he had contrived at last to make comfortable for himself, and pulling cords for windows and ventilators, she had squared her chin, saying, "Now I'll go. I know I can trust you not to tire the patient or stay too long," and had herself left them.

At once, Carey had turned his face to Miss Pomfret and said (he seemed to have to make an effort, she had thought, even to speak), "Mary, my old friend, I'm a dying man. I know. It is only a matter of hours, not of days. . . . So I wanted to see you once again, to thank you for everything you've done for me, always . . . and to ask you one question. . . . You've seen so much of the course of my life: do you recognize this room?" . . . And then, as she looked round, she had understood; the enamelled cornices and doors, the distempered walls, the metal furniture, had taken on other colours, other lines. A gold-lacquered paper flowered again over the walls, a Chinese screen stood in front of the door, a Symphony in White, by Whistler, hung over the mantelpiece (now filled in, to hold an electric heater). In the far corner, on the muffled piano, stood rows of silver-framed photographs of Forelli in the roles of Carmen, La Sonnambula, Lucia and a hundred other operatic heroines, or of mellifluous male singers decked for their parts, and on the tables, the vases of sick-room flowers had been ousted for the instant by vast, formal trophies of roses, orchids and lilies. . . . He lay now dying in the very room of the very house in which his life had been crowned and consumed.

He told her that he had fought—as she had been certain he would—against the idea of leaving Albany at all. But the doctor had ordered him to be taken at once in a motor-ambulance to his favourite nursing-home. Carey had not even been told where it was situated, and had felt too ill to ask questions. On arrival, when the old atmosphere had begun to distil itself round him in the room, he had felt sure that this was the result of his fever: but during the night, as he lay awake there, he had become convinced, on the contrary, of its reality. And a curious mingled sense of comfort and inquietude had assailed him. . . . However, the slight effort of describing his feelings evidently tired him out, and as he seemed to be growing sleepy, Miss Pomfret had soon left him.

Next morning she had returned again to see him. But this time he did not know her. . . . He was apparently talking Italian to someone on the other side of the bed. She tried to make out what he was saying, but it was no use: she only knew a few words of Italian. Then he fell silent again, intent, as though listening.

True Lovers' Knot

... And was it her imagination, she wondered, or did she really distinguish just for a moment, a coloratura trill, high up and far away, almost out of hearing? ... She wished her ears had been sharper, for it sounded, oh beautiful; heavenly, you might say.

Probably it was a gramophone or wireless somewhere near by. You couldn't get away from them nowadays. But she was never sure.

Touching Wood

I do not yet know how this story ends: for what I am going to tell you happened only yesterday morning, before I left the boat at Suez.

With a pile of books and an empty soup-cup beside me, I sat in a deck-chair, staring out into mist-edged nothingness, where not even a dolphin or a flying-fish leapt for the diversion of the passengers. Everything seemed to be warm and damp, very damp. The edge of the sky was hung with ragged banners of cloud, and the edge of the sea melted into it. My neighbour, also with several books by his side, and one lying open upon his knee, stared, with a similar fixity, into the watery, empty perspective. The vast melancholy of the sea— only supportable because of the laziness it engenders,

and of the manner in which it causes one day to tele-
scope into another, inducing in many persons the subsequent conviction that they must have enjoyed the
voyage, for the time to have passed so quickly—hung
over both of us: that much was clear. Tall, thin and
with rather fine hands, my neighbour displayed in his
physique an unusual sensitiveness, and I wondered,
idly, who he was. . . . The books afforded no clue, for
they were of several sorts; a translation of the Greek
Anthology, a novel by P. G. Wodehouse, Dunne's *Experiment in Time,* a new biography of some dead poli-
tician by Mr. Harold Nicolson, a volume of short stories
by the late D. H. Lawrence, and—I noticed now—one
of my own books, *The Man Who Lost Himself.* Suddenly he turned his eyes from the water and addressed
me.

"Do you like the sea?" he asked.

"Yes, I love it, in a way," I answered, "in spite of the
boredom—and, with me, alas, of the terror. For I'm
quite a good sailor: but when other people are lying in
their bunks, wishing they could drown, I'm lying on
mine, praying that I shan't, and thinking in terror of
the endless, undulating depths beneath. That's why I
prefer the Mediterranean, where you can usually see
land. . . . But it seems to have disappeared altogether
to-day. . . . Or, better still, give me the Suez Canal; I
look forward to an enjoyable afternoon."

"Oh, I know: I'm a bit like that myself," he said. "In fact, as you're a writer, I'll tell you a story about it. But I hope you're not superstitious?

"Perhaps you can hardly call it a story, really," he added; "it's an illustration, more than a story, or the proof of a theory. . . . And in this instance the theory or the moral is the old, obvious one, which D. H. Lawrence was so fond of emphasizing that what you *feel* is—and must always be—more true than what you merely think: judge by touch, as it were, rather than sight. But people don't have the courage nowadays to act on what they feel: they act by reason, and then try to invent rational explanations afterwards, of the singular things that happen to them. But it's no use: no use at all.

"The ship, bound for South America, left Tilbury on a wet December afternoon: but the next day and for two days afterwards the sea, even when we crossed the Bay of Biscay, resembled a blue summer lake. In spite of the calm, though, we were late in arriving at Lisbon, while, once there, the interminable arrangements of the harbour authorities seemed specially calculated to make us later still in leaving it. I stood, watching the departing passengers, and listening to a fierce Portuguese quarrel that spluttered like a damp firework, between the ship's agent and an official of the custom-house. . . . There were only two new arrivals of whom to take notice, an Englishwoman and her husband. She was certainly beautiful in a curious way, like one of the Fates. Her eyes, wide open, had the blue depths of an oracle, in which many meanings, one true and many false, could be read. There was something classical, or pre-classical, about that startled and stony visage, something of Cassandra, and of the doom of the whole House of Atreus. . . . Something, too, I thought—or should I say, I felt—at the time, of a mermaid: for her eyes belonged to the sea. . . . And yet it was at Mycenae, in the broken palace above the deep ravine, on that hill which seems to be alone for ever with the sea and the sky, as though they were washing it free of that doom, and the taint that caused it, that she would have been, I think, most at home. . . . Beside her, her husband looked pleasantly matter-of-fact; but it was only her appearance which was unusual: her clothes seemed specially designed to destroy the particular kind of beauty she possessed, to degrade it and make it ordinary.

"The following morning, sitting on deck, as we are now, I found myself next to them, and, after playing for a little with our books in the listless manner which the movement and vibration of all ships—for there is a very strong link between sea-sickness and print—enforce, we began to talk a little. . . . They gave an ordinary enough impression, too, when they spoke, and her

voice—quiet, busy, comfortable, though rather empty—
had no element in it of either prophecy or tragedy.
. . . And yet I knew, I felt, I was *aware*—informed, I
suppose, by the exploring of those antennae which so
much excel the faculties of the mind—that, somehow
or other, she was inextricably associated with these
qualities. . . . We talked in a desultory manner for two
hours or more, and during the whole of that time the
sea, which had been up till now so unruffled—even in
those latitudes where you would have expected it to be
at its most swelling and boisterous—began indubitably
to show increasing symptoms of a change of mood. It
felt as though it were trying out its powers, though
only, as yet, with some future occasion in view. Little
winds whistled in the corners, and there was a roll on
the boat that caused the usual jokes and laughter
among the younger passengers, trampling noisily round
the deck, and instilled in the players of quoits and
other games a desire to be more hearty and jolly than
ever, in order to cover up a certain incipient queasiness.
. . . You ask what we'd been talking about? . . . Well,
I forget, but all sorts of things, politics and books—safe,
dull books—and travel.

"With every minute, though, conversation became
more difficult, for there were sounds of things crashing
from time to time, and the wind howled ever more
loudly, even though ours was a comparatively sheltered

corner. . . . They were going, she told me, to Buenos Ayres—or 'B-A,' as she called it, with her affectation of ordinariness—for the voyage, weren't even going on shore for a day or two at Rio. No, a week at 'B-A,' and then straight back home; 'that's the place for us,' she said. Mr. Ruevinny—for that was their name—had been ill, it appeared, and had been ordered this voyage by the doctor. 'I tried to persuade my wife not to come,' he explained, 'but she insisted. I didn't persuade you to come, did I, darling?' he added, turning to her, 'I did everything I could to stop it.'

"No, I don't recall the whole conversation with any distinctness: only one or two things like that. I remember Mrs. Ruevinny saying, in her practical, putting-up-with-no-nonsense and yet singularly empty voice—a voice which said things as though it did not mean them—'Well, I'm a fatalist: you can't escape what's coming to you—so there you are! You must make the best of it. No fox can escape for long, if the pack is out after him.' . . . I recollect that very well, for at the moment this remark—so ordinary, one to which we have all had to listen against our wills so often—irritated me almost beyond endurance. It accorded so ill, I thought, with that curious beauty, with that face which seemed waiting for one of the great emotions—and it was *fear,* I felt sure—to make it a supreme vehicle of expression. . . . But one is so often disappointed with people in that way, by their enunciating sentiments which do not suit them. . . . Then she went on to talk of bazaars in the home counties, and gave way to little bursts of self-importance, equally inappropriate.

"And yet were they, I wondered at the time, in reality bursts of self-importance? She brought them into the conversation, I felt, not so much to impress a stranger as to comfort herself. Because such functions belonged to everyday life, as a rule lacking in both heroism and disaster, just as the opinions she voiced were the opinions of everyday life: and she clung to them, I felt, because she was desperately anxious to impress upon herself that life was really of this pattern for her, and that some dim, huge existence of antique catastrophe, to which she belonged, and from which she had once fled, possessed no actuality. Every opinion she uttered, every occasion to which she referred, was as though she pinched herself to be sure that she was awake, and that the nightmare had passed. . . . So, I felt, might one of the Atridae, Clytemnestra or Elektra, in the intervals of those catastrophic events to which their names are, to us, indissolubly attached, have told acquaintances of the Sale of Work she was getting up, in order to aid the honest poor of Mycenae.

"Rougher and rougher it grew; and I did not see them again that day. Certainly it had grown too stormy now for one to take any sort of pleasure in the voyage.

Open the Door!

It was not even possible to sleep: though storms, as a rule, make me feel sleepy: and at night, if for a single moment you dozed off, you were sure to be woken at once by the flying open, flapping and slamming of cupboard doors, or by the sensation that the soul itself, the *psyche* round which the body is built up, had slightly shifted its habitation. . . . 'Why,' all the passengers, as so often during a voyage, were asking themselves: '*why* did I do it?' . . . But my own chief emotion, and one that I nearly always experience on the Atlantic, though it has been my lot to travel a good deal upon it, was of fright: I did not feel sick, I felt frightened of those cold, dark valleys beneath, as deep, we are told, as the island mountains are high. . . . Incidentally (forgive me for interrupting my own story) but hasn't it grown much rougher since we began talking, or is it my imagination?"

I had to admit that the weather had changed. The boat had begun to pitch about in an unexpected way.

"I thought so," he said, and paused a moment. "Still, it will at least be smooth in the Canal. . . . But let me proceed," he continued. "Fortunately I was leaving the boat at Madeira, and that was only two days ahead. But how sincerely during those hours I longed for it, that nest of purple bougainvillea and peroxide blondes, poised in mid-ocean under its cosy of Atlantic cloud.

"The next day was of too unpleasant a character for

one to be able to take an interest in anything, in food or drink or sleep or passengers: but I noticed, all the same, that Mr. Ruevinny was alone at luncheon. . . . The following morning the storm appeared to have abated a little, though not much, and, while walking up and down the deck, I met him.

" 'Good morning!' I cried, with false sea-heartiness. 'And how are *you* this morning? . . . I'm sorry to see you're alone.'

" 'Yes, it's a nuisance,' he replied. 'I had so much hoped it would be fine. . . . After all, we're getting near Madeira now, and it oughtn't to be like this. . . . I tell you, it worries me. . . . You see, it isn't so much that my wife's a bad sailor—she doesn't really feel ill now; the truth is, she's frightened in a ship!'

" 'That's nothing to be ashamed of,' I said. 'I am, too. . . . I believe a good many people are, if only they'd allow themselves to admit it.'

" 'I dare say. . . . But you see, it's different for her: the last time she was on a proper voyage was in the *Titanic:* her twin brother went down with it, and she was only rescued herself by a miracle. . . . Why, for years she wouldn't go abroad at all, even refused to take on the hour's journey across the Channel; though, before that, she used to love Paris. . . And I'll tell you a peculiar thing; the sea can be as smooth as anything, and the moment she sets her foot on board, sure enough, it begins to get stormy: I've seen it happen in the Channel, scores of times, so that often I wished I hadn't persuaded her to change her mind and come with me, even for that short distance. . . . I ought never to have let her come on this journey: never: I ought to have forbidden it absolutely, from the start. . . . But she had been worrying about me—I'd been ill a long time, and those damned medicos said a long sea voyage was the only thing to put me right—and she insisted. I couldn't stop her: it seemed as though she *must* come, although she dreaded it, if you can get my meaning.' . . . So that was it! . . . no wonder she was frightened, even at the surface level. I thought of the magnificent ship on her maiden voyage, of the two bands playing, and of that sudden ice-cold crash, and silence, as the breath of destruction reached it; and then of the watery confusion, of the strange, voiceless last meetings in those green alleys between the waves, where those who could swim bobbed up and down; or were knocked together like corks, but, their voices being lost already beneath the sound of the ocean, could not communicate in any way, and so, it must have seemed, had become hostile to each other. . . . So that was it! . . . That was the meaning in those wide-open eyes, like the eyes of a statue in bright sunlight: that was the meaning, perhaps subconscious, under her casual, silly yet intent words, 'No fox can escape for long, if the pack is out after him.' . . . No, nor a human being, if the whole pack of furies attend his coming and his going.

"That afternoon we arrived at Madeira, and I said good-bye. The Ruevinnys—beset though they were on deck by the islanders, who were trying to sell them embroideries, flowers, sandals, boxes of palm-wood, models of bullock-carts, native dresses and budgerigars— waved to me as I left for the shore in a motor-boat: and I noticed, again, the singular lack of expression in her face, which yet showed, when once you comprehended, so much more terror than terror itself. She gave a look, too, I thought, of longing towards the land: but I was too far away to see clearly. . . . At any rate, they should be all right now. The rest of the journey, especially at this time of year, should be one of tropical calm, of deep, blue phosphorescent gardens beneath the waters, and of flying-fishes leaping over them as birds skim a lawn.

"It was not until a fortnight later, not until a fortnight after it had happened, that I saw the newspaper: '*Hurricane in South Atlantic Seas. Coastline Towns Swept by Tidal Wave,*' I read. '*British Liner Sinks Off Rio. All Lives Lost.*' I thought at once of Mrs. Ruevinny. . . . So it was over now. . . . She belonged in some way to the sea, and it must reclaim her: she had always known that, I reflected, even though she could not always rationally believe it. At any rate, it was over, whatever it might mean: the end of some long pursuit, of which one could not tell the beginning: or, perhaps —who knows?—it was only the middle act of a drama laid over several centuries, or epochs. . . . I wondered how that lovely face had looked at the end, and knowing what was in store for her, how much more matter-of-fact she had contrived to make her voice, when she talked to her husband for the last time? . . . And yet, as so often happens, actuality and its foretelling had been a little at odds. . . . I turned over to the stop-press news. *'Survivor Rescued,'* I read. *'Strange Coincidence.* . . . Mrs. Ruevinny, who was rescued yesterday afternoon in a state of exhaustion, proves to be one of the survivors of the *Titanic:* her twin brother perished with the ship. It is feared that Mr. Ruevinny, well known in the sporting world, and all the other passengers and hands are lost.' . . . So it had not got her after all: the fox was free once more. The last act, poor woman, had not been played.

". . . I suppose you'd call it superstitious of me to feel like that? But life sometimes seems easier to understand, if one is superstitious. . . . Well, that was thirteen years ago. . . . And, touching wood, she's on this ship, bound for Ceylon to see her son. (I spoke to her this morning: doesn't look a day older.) But what ought one to do, act on superstitious belief or defy it? . . .

Somehow I lack the courage to do anything so silly as leave the boat at Suez."

He stopped talking, and became silent, pondering: while I, though obliged to hold on to everything I saw in order to keep my balance, managed to get downstairs to send a cable.

Defeat

Battle alters the face of the world, but defeat and collapse may at first leave it intact, just as a gutted house often shows no change, except for its dead, blank windows. . . . So it was with the little town of Château Vignal, formerly so prosperous. Ruin and chaos were implicit in it, but, at first sight, did not show themselves. Its structure was bony and enduring, and its grey-white streets ran from either side of the Loire like ribs from the backbone of a carcase. The trams still creaked down narrow alleys under the overhanging sculpture of Gothic churches; in the one broad boulevard the shops still boasted displays of goods at high prices; fruits and vegetables lay heaped up in baskets, level with the knees of the old peasant women who sold them, under the hot and radiant sunshine of the open market and, though meat, sugar, spices were unprocurable, other, younger peasant women carried hens under their arms and cackled to each other across the struggling, feathered bodies. Beneath the large, glossy-leaved trees on which magnolias, large and white as the soup-bowls of the alms-houses near by, were flowering sweetly, the local idiot still sat slobbering in the empty public-garden. The only change noticeable was that the tramps, who usually slept here at night, were now seeking escape during the day-time and formed those almost inconjecturable mounds of rags, lifeless save for a slight nearly imperceptible heaving, which could be seen lying in several directions upon the yellowing grass. The fishermen still lined the banks of the river, with its high, and as it seemed at this season, unnecessary stone walls, and one or two, more intrepid, stood in the water up to their knees. (Indeed, owing to the scarcity of provisions, there were, perhaps, more of them, and they were even more patient.) The cafés were still open, too, though the regular clients were ruffled at being unable to obtain their favourite drinks, and in the chief café the band of four ancient men in dinner-jackets still played "Selections from *Carmen*," the "Barcarolle," and various waltzes, and a woman singer, in a pink evening dress, and carrying

Defeat

with her the invisible prestige attaching to many diplomas from many provincial *conservatoires,* still sang the Jewel Song from *Faust* and various well-known airs from the operas of Puccini.

Little change manifested itself, nevertheless the poison of defeat ran through the corpus of the people in the same manner in which a poison circulates through the body with its blood, by the aid of its own blood. And the outward form that the poison took during this stage, which resembled the unconsciousness of a patient, broken by fits of delirium, was a chaotic, meaningless placidity, relief at the coming of a peace that did not exist, varied by sudden spasms of virulently anti-foreign, and especially anti-British, sentiment. But this xenophobia did not extend toward the conquerors. The German officers, the German soldiers were even regarded momentarily with a certain admiration, a certain wonder at their hard, mechanical bearing and efficiency, and the women of the town looked at them more curiously, and longer, than at their own men, yet covered, many of them, with dust, slouching past impassively in twos and threes, unshaven, silent, vacant-eyed, puffing at cigarettes that never left their lips even when they exchanged a few words.

It was a Sunday afternoon. On the terrace of the public-gardens, under the delicate fluttering of acacia leaves, the usual Sunday family groups, the usual Sunday combinations—like a family tree in reverse—of grandfather, grandmothers, uncles, aunts, parents, all in dark clothes, with, as their culmination, a single, small, pale child, wandered and stared without purpose, and from the interior of the Café de l'Univers came the familiar dull crack of billiard balls and shuttered laughter. Vanished were the Algerian, Moroccan and Tunisian troops who usually lent colour to the scene, but at a few tables some French soldiers were playing cards, and at another sat a captain in the French army, the young girl to whom he was engaged, and her mother. . . . Not far away, near the entrance from the public-gardens and divided from it by the usual line of green boxes containing nameless evergreen shrubs, a German officer, with a creased neck, ox-eyes, a monocle, and a tunic that appeared to contain a wooden body, was consuming a *bock*.

The Captain did not look at him. He had only returned home yesterday. His eyes were entirely reserved for his younger companion, the daughter of Doctor Dorien; in a way she was pretty, but her essential correctness, the result in conjunction of a convent upbringing and the inherited burgess virtues of her home, her clothes, with the typical dowdy *chic* of the French provincial town, and her carefully coiffured hair, all combined to impart to her an air of insipidity, of garnished emptiness, as though she had long been prepared, and was still waiting, for the vital forces to descend and give her life. Her smile, on the other hand, was quick and alert, and her eyes soon warmed, soon lost their emptiness and gained fire.

The face of the Captain, sensitive and, in spite of the several ribbons he was wearing, almost feminine in fineness of cut and expression, was drawn and exhausted, for he had only stopped fighting three days before, and within him his soul was dead. Notwithstanding, the bond that united him to Estelle, that mutual but indefinable flow of sympathy which seemed to pour into every cell of each body from the other, comforted him. They had been friends from childhood, and their marriage had been arranged since their earliest infancy. . . . Perhaps theirs was not love in the romantic sense, but, from the Latin approach, it constituted love. On his side composed of tenderness, affection and physical desire, on hers it rose out of her respect for his qualities of command and valour and from a need for mental and physical subservience. He fully appreciated the nature of it, that Estelle looked up to him, and he was relieved to find that this feeling of hers still persisted after what had happened. . . . But he knew it was just, because he was no coward and, where many brave men had been routed, he had stood his ground.

He realized—and she had been able to make him

realize—that this respect for his valour, like his valour itself, had suffered no diminution from defeat—"defeat." He supposed it must be because he was so tired, but through the tinkling phrases of the Delibes ballet music now being played, the words "defeat," "defeat," "defeat" drummed in his ears, and with his inner eye he still watched—and, he thought, would watch eternally—the armoured columns advancing, those immense and senseless machines, trundling and thundering along at a rate no Frenchman could have anticipated, could still see them, hear them, crushing the heads of men like nuts ground under the heel, could still see the cowering, surging waves of humanity upon the roads, the household goods, upon barrows and carts, the clocks and trunks and vases, for better protection covered beneath the best mattress, could still see the old women and the ill left behind, fallen in the ditches beneath the grey and suffocating hedges, could still hear the nearing remorseless thunder, and rattling machine-gun fire, from the dive-bombers, swarming above the civilian crowds, scattering them and rounding them up as they ran hither and thither, all wearing, as though in self-protection, the sheep-coloured, shameful livery of the dust. Such sights and sounds were as yet more real to him than the silvery perspective of tall, shivering poplars and flowing river, its cool islands of willow and tamarisk lying like full baskets of feathers upon the water, upon which his glance rested, and were not far from him even when he gazed into the calm and limpid brown depths of Estelle's eyes.

He must pretend to be the same or it might shock her. . . . But he knew that he had changed, and the world with him, and he wished the band would not continually play the old, gay melodies of a dead life; it was like seeing the ghost of someone you had loved. . . . *"Defeat."* . . . And yet there were in it certain pleasant prospects, though tinged with the year's shame. The war, a bad war, badly begun, had stopped. His men would no longer be slaughtered. Above all, his marriage, hitherto delayed, firstly by the previous economic collapse and then by the war, could take place almost immediately, their parents agreed. And their old affection remained steadfast. . . . But sometimes he almost wished that the kind of affection he read in her eyes, that respect for a man who was brave and could command, had ceased to exist, replaced by some other kindred but more reasonable sentiment; for of what use was courage, individual courage, now, against this armoured mass, how could flesh pit itself against iron?

Meanwhile their conversation, albeit desultory, was, on the surface, gay enough. They avoided all mention of the war, but teased one another and preened themselves like any other young couple in ordinary times. They discussed how they would live after their marriage, and seemed to forget for some time the presence of her mother, and then, all at once, to remember it and try to make amends. All three of them made their cakes and *tisane*—for there was no coffee—last as long a time as possible.

"Remember, I shall have to find a trade now," the Captain said, "I shall no longer be in the army. I shall have to get up every morning to go to the office, and probably my temper will be very bad, for I am not used to it. . . . And you will have to prepare for my home-coming, and walk back so that I get air, or otherwise I shall take the tram to be with you the sooner, and so shall soon grow old and fat." (Her face fell, he noticed, when he told her that he would leave the army; evidently she had not fully grasped that the French army was in dissolution.) "And I shall dine every night with you and Maman," he continued, taking the older woman into the conversation, "but I shall be very cross unless you both give me the food I like." (But, inside his head the words "defeat," "defeat" sounded like advancing columns.)

"And what about *me?*" Estelle answered; "you will have to study me now, and come home early so as to be with me. If you leave the regiment, there will be no talk of being 'on duty,' or of 'having to dine in the Officers' Mess.' . . . No excuses will exist any more."

But all this talk, he felt, meant so little. Like the

scene itself, it was curiously on the surface, with no shades or undertones. The sun glowed down now through the acacia leaves, seeming to consume them, and rested full on the faces round them. The woman in the pink evening dress had, amid much applause, stopped singing, and conversation and laughter swelled up from the tables.

Then the band struck up again, a waltz, the "Wiener Wald" by Johann Strauss. . . . Hardly a place empty. . . . A party of four or five gaping soldiers came in, near the entrance by which the German officer was sitting. They passed him, and came toward the Captain; they dragged their feet, were dishevelled and untidy, talked loudly and smoked cigarettes. He recognized them; they were men who for long had served under him, but they stared at him idly, without saluting, and slouched past him to a table beyond. They were noisy, but possessed the very look of men who have lost all spirit, except a new will to insolence. (*"Defeat"*: this was defeat.) He looked away and did not glance at Estelle, fixing his eyes upon the distance, where the water rippled by the edge of rushes and flowering clumps of yellow iris. . . . But, suddenly, a guttural sound obtruded and made him take notice. (The conversation stopped at the neighbouring tables, though the aproned waiters continued to perform their clever acts of equilibrium, with arms poised and trays uplifted above the heads of their customers, in the manner of jugglers.) It was the German officer, summoning and beckoning to the men; the Captain's men. Now they pulled themselves together. Their false aggressiveness ebbed away and they filed back solemnly and saluted the foreigner, as he bade them.

"Now go back and salute your Captain," the enemy continued in his thick, distorted French.

The men sheepishly did as they were told. . . . The Captain acknowledged their salute in the customary manner, nonchalantly and as though at his ease, and his soldiers returned to their table. . . . *Defeat,* defeat, this was defeat, and the world lay broken round him. He felt, perceived immediately that nothing in his own life would ever be the same again. This incident had transformed Estelle's view of him, and her new attitude toward him was defined and without the possibility of retrieval: it was final; he knew it, deep in his bones. The bond had snapped. Never now would they be married. It was as though for her the virtue had gone out of him. His manhood lay shattered for both of them, wrecked by the clumsy courtesy, or, who could tell? the cruel courtesy of a victor. . . . But he was tired, so tired that he scarcely suffered. It was over.

Plague=Cart before Horse

Now the flights of pigeons that executed their strange symphonies far above us—for each bird had tied to its body a wooden whistle—had stopped their music. The sky had become an immense blue dome, deepening in colour, and no wings seemed to be beating in it, or against it. . . . The evening belonged to the first spring heats, and the air was scented with the lilac, which in this climate had sprung to blossom in a day. We sat out in the courtyard, five of us, talking and drinking cool drinks, and to us, through the immediate and outlying silence, reached the cries and sounds of a great Chinese city; cries and sounds which were to continue without ceasing, drums and gongs and bells and wooden clappers (no one who has not visited China can imagine the variety of sounds that wood striking wood can produce), each one denoting a trade—peddler or juggler or mountebank or fortune-teller—until the morning, when the terrible anthem of the pigs being killed, thousands of them having their throats cut at the same moment, would complete the concert.

The talk, like one of the kites that could here in the day-time be seen zigzagging up into the sky, veered hither and thither, first touching on people in general, thence to criminals, to crime—and then on to what part, as it were, the scenery might play in the drama. ... I had seen, I said, in a far, dead island in the western Mediterranean, a house which had the reputation of being cursed: in every generation some terrible, irremediable event occurred within its precincts. This miniature palace lay nestling only a little way above the tideless blue sea that lapped the very foot of the garden; a very beautiful, pink marble, eighteenth-century house, surrounded by giant olive trees and by palms. On its scented terraces, broken and crumbling, brooded the doomed, Latin decadence of D'Annunzio's novels; here mother killed son in one generation, and brother killed brother in the next. And the criminals whom this little sea-palace bred were handsome and noble, terrible in their crimes. Through the hot days and nights the house smouldered in that dark wood by the sea. There was nothing gloomy about it, only something infinitely passionate, and beautiful, but indefinably wicked, so that it was impossible not to wonder whether, at least in this instance, the house had not in reality influenced its inhabitants toward their various cruel deeds and inexorable fates, rather than that the inhabitants had influenced their shell? . . . This delicate, pale rose-coloured dwelling, so elegant, so lovely in proportion and design, was yet an expression of the dark and ancient soil out of which it had grown; its strength—one had almost written "virtue"—rested in the earth in which it was rooted—and what strange histories haunt that luxuriant, desolate shore! . . . Thus it may be that, if a modern palace were built at Mycenae, on that tremendous and terrible hill, the Furies would come to life again, ride through its halls and rush through the ravine, till the air would sweep shuddering up in them for a moment, as now the tops of the trees, after the aeroplanes have passed, cower down from the mimic, very icy breath of doom. . . . So, too, the peace that pervades many monastic dwellings, even though, long secularized, they have sunk to being hotels, may be due more to the structure and its site than to the monks who made them. Why, for example, had they chosen this position?—because it was, to their minds, blessed. Why, before that, had a temple stood here, and what spirit inspired the humble, whitewashed yet aspiring beauty of their design, fitting as closely to the rock, and belonging to it as much as a barnacle to a ship's bottom? Similarly with these now domesticated temples near us in the Western Hills, with their sweet wistarias, their apple trees in flower, their pools and slanting eaves; the Buddhist priests had surely chosen them because their outlook influenced the mind towards peace and virtue?

Christopher Standish took on the argument in a different, more material vein, telling us, from his medical experience at Liverpool and in industrial Lancashire, how typhus can haunt the soil, so that the ground may never be cleared of infection. Thus a slum could be destroyed, and a new palace erected instead; yet, however many times the buildings on this site were burnt or pulled down, the typhus would inevitably return. . . . But then, this disease is carried by vermin, and vermin can survive fire, and sword, and even sanitation: (think of the gaol-fever that used to make English prisons such haunted and horrible places of incarceration, attacking even at times the judges and the juries, so that it seemed as though this fever, born of criminals, were seeking to enact a revenge for them upon society). . . . Such fevers are intelligible; nevertheless, it would perhaps be true, he thought, to say that typhus haunted the site of such a building. . . . Standish became silent, and again the cries and various metallic musical sounds of the night reached us. A fortune-teller was tapping his way down the lane outside, and one could hear the creaking wheels of the carts; (so, in England, centuries ago, must have sounded the plague-carts as they creaked through the streets of the city at midnight, their husky drivers crying, "Bring out your dead!").

Now Angus Rockingham struck up for the first time. "I suppose you will think that it is putting the cart before the horse," he said, "but somehow it seems to fit what you are saying. . . . You know that before I came out here, I was in Cyprus. I lived there for five years; in that outpost of empire, where every day in the broiling heat the British visitor takes off his topee, and eats roast beef and steak-and-kidney pudding, roly-poly, and then, as an offering to local colour, devours a viscous, melting square of Turkish delight, to the accompaniment of sticky, sweet wines; the only Greek island with no Greek statues, no Greek temples, no shape to its landscape; nothing except its one, incomparable Bel Paese—a French Gothic building, flowering in a beautiful but inapposite position—and a few, as they seem, whitewashed English parish churches masquerading as mosques. The natives, too—you must call them natives—are for the most part not Greek, but descended from the slave races of Roman times, dirty, stupid, cringing and for ever unfortunate. . . . However, you won't want to hear my views about Cyprus, for whenever an English paper reaches us, you always read that it is the Jewel of the Empire. Further, I lived, admittedly, in the most beautiful part of the island; in an ancient Turkish city some three miles from the sea. There, at least, as one walked by the tideless, deep-blue waters, something of Greece lingered. Although there were no temples, not even a pillar of them surviving, the shore was lined with fragments of marble walls and pavements, and with shells that seemed, equally, to be the work of some great, long-dead architect. Acanthus and asphodel grew from the broken, shapeless masonry, and anemones turned their fluttering eyes to the sun from any bank where there was soil: and any bank where there was soil indicated foundations lying buried beneath it. . . . On the surface, there was neither ancient, nor any modern, buildings: at least, only one, a large, unused, melancholy-looking low structure, with the damp-stained plaster peeling from its walls. . . . It had been built as a smallpox hospital some twenty years before, I found out: and then, since smallpox here had been eradicated and extinguished—that much, at least, is to our credit—had, for some reason or other, never been adapted to any other purpose, had remained virgin and desolate—though as for that, had it been used, the desolation would, I thought, have been of the very same kind. In this climate—for so far as I could see no attention had been paid to the fabric—it had remained marvellously whole. Flowering weeds grew on the roof, but the roof itself was still perfect.

"I have said that the building was desolate, but this does not mean that I want you to think that it was ugly: it was not ugly. On the contrary, it was spacious and well-constructed, standing upon an exquisite site; a poem, as it were, a *fleur du mal* in brick and plaster. The government official who had designed it must surely have been a genius, for, with the little money at his disposal, he had summed up the idea of illness in general and smallpox in particular. Just as Vanbrugh piled up Blenheim Palace into a triumphal ode for the Great Captain's victories, so this obscure, perhaps unconscious, artist had made out of his rather pitiful materials an absolute expression, a personification of smallpox, that horrible and disfiguring disease. . . . Not for a moment could you have mistaken it for a prison, nor even for an ordinary isolation hospital. No: smallpox was expressed in its every aspect. It seemed dedicated, in some way, to the development and flowering of this particular plague. Long before I knew its history, I had formed a correct conclusion—as it turned out—concerning its original purpose.

"After I had been there for a year or two, a merchant retired from Bombay came to settle in the town with his wife and children. It was cheap and warm, and after a long sojourn in the East he could not support the English climate. . . . But even here, life was difficult: he was never well, he could not find a house, and he did not like the only hotel in the town. (Indeed this was not surprising, for the Cyprus hotel combines the worst points of the English inn and the Turkish caravan-serai. . . .) The arrival of the Verskills was a great comfort to me, for I was growing more and more tired of the place, and the family afforded me pleasant companionship. I quickly formed a friendship with Clare, the daughter: a lovely girl and worthy of better things. Her charm, like that of her brothers, was obvious, and consisted in her vitality and health and good spirits. . . . But all the same she was charming, and charged with an energy delightful in this environment. I don't think any of them had much imagination, but they possessed the good nature of all things that are young and healthy.

"Certainly the father was not imaginative, yet he allowed the town to get on his nerves. He could not bear the system of life he found in the hotel here, for he was used to being master of a house. . . . And then one day, walking among the deserted foundations of temples, down paths, lined with asphodel and acanthus, that had once been great roads, he saw this low building I have described and, in his dismal, discontented fashion, fell in love with it. He liked its air of space. Perhaps he even liked its air of loneliness—in any case, with his family about him, he could never be lonely. Servants were easy to secure in Cyprus, though difficult, perhaps, to drill; and he could run it. It would give him something to do. He, rather than his wife, that placid, silent woman, would assume the organization of the house, inside and out; he would draw up charts for the servants, so that they should know when to get up, and what to do. As for the outside, he would decorate this terrace with geraniums (they grew here as easily as wild flowers), and there he would plant a grove of fruit trees, so that 'the Missis' could make her jams again, as she had long years ago in England. . . . I tried—I hardly know why, except that I liked Clare— to dissuade him, invented reasons for not taking the house, said it was damp, and that the provincial government would not sell it. It was silly of me, for after all there was nothing against it—there had never been a case of illness there. However, my arguments were of no avail; the authorities responded more quickly than usual, and, in spite of my pleading, Mr. Verskill acquired his bargain, and was delighted with it. . . . Here it is only fair to say that, to my surprise, he made his new dwelling, in his own way, charming and agreeable. It became much less depressing, seemed to have come into its own. The colours were cool and gay, the furniture quiet and very English. Even the fruit trees didn't look out of place, and I much enjoyed sitting out in the garden of an evening with the family. . . . I dined there, I remember, the last night before my leave.

"When I returned," he continued, "they were dead, all dead of smallpox; the first cases in the island for twenty years. . . . And do you know, such a massacre, a family of five, and eight servants, lacked the poignance of an individual tragedy? It is never the same. Just as revolutions and wars leave no—or very few— ghosts, compared with murders, so this catastrophe left little shadow behind it. . . . This is not to say that I did not miss them; I could never bear to pass that way. But sometimes I had to. . . . The house, I suppose, had been fumigated; the windows were shut and barred, the eyes closed again; no air ever blew in. Poor Clare!"

His voice trailed away, to be lost in the sounds of the Chinese night, drums and gongs and bells and wooden clappers, sounds that would continue until the morning; when the terrible anthem of the pigs being killed, thousands of them having their throats cut simultaneously, would complete the concert.

A Stereoscopic Story in Two Parts

Pompey and Some Peaches—I

Old Mulready Maure had been at one time the leading English art critic. He had known every great figure of his period. But when he retired to the gaunt country house near York whence he had originally emerged, his neighbours complained that this lean, angular, quixotic man was a bore. Stories of Rossetti and Whistler, of Swinburne and Morris, meant nothing to these faces that looked permanently "blooded," indelibly tainted with the smear from the fox's brush. Though my nature prompts me to dislike critics, seeing in them members of the opposite team in the game of Gentlemen *v.* Players or Foxes *v.* Birds of Paradise, I liked listening to the old man's talk, and it was he who first told me, one day when I went to see him, the story about the peaches.

"Even towards the end of Dubosque's life, you could have bought a picture of his, not for a song, but for the mere trouble of crying 'Rags and Bones' out in the street. Whereas now that he's dead (where the dealers wanted to get him), only a millionaire can afford to *look* at his work, let alone buy it.

"And what an extraordinary man he was, what an extraordinary painter, more particularly for an Englishman!

"Some great artists construct, like Rubens or Titian or Tiepolo or Delacroix, their own gigantic and overwhelming lands of fantasy, new Indies of the imagination upon whose shores men have never yet set foot: others, like Rembrandt or Chardin or Cézanne, reveal a world equally new, whether dark or glittering with light, within the most familiar objects. And it was to this last, perhaps almost rarer division that Richard Dubosque belonged.

"In appearance, as well as in the way in which he approached the art of painting, he resembled much more a Frenchman than an Englishman, and, as his name showed, he was of French blood; I believe, Huguenot. Even before he came to live up here, the life he led was extremely ascetic. By that, I don't mean that as a young man he had not had his fling, for he was full of temperament, but that his life was dedicated: his desire to paint ousted every other passion, and he would rather look at a glass of Margaux, let us say, and study it, than drink it. But the austerity of his life compared strangely with the greed—if you see what I mean—of his painting, in which I always felt a sense of consuming appetite. No French master, not even Cézanne, possessed a more complete understanding of material objects, a greater feeling for their texture, their volume and the unseeable—if I may phrase it like that—organization of the interior as expressed by their contour and surface. With his painting of an apple, for instance, he seemed to tell us everything that was known, not only of this particular apple, but of every other apple in the world, and by the voluptuousness of its presentation it was plain that Eve had confided to him the secret hissed into her ear by the serpent. That is what gave him his unique place in English art; he painted objects, material objects, as only a lover could paint them.

"He did not really like painting people, his life was too much occupied by his painting, and he had no wish for distraction. And so his cottage up here on the wolds suited him perfectly. It was a dear little rough, white-walled house, with a garden divided into four compartments by box hedges, and with a wall of loose stones enclosing it, an oasis in the vast prospect. This was his part of the country too, and he loved it and understood it, and the fact that the nearest village to his home was five or six miles away, appealed to him as a positive advantage. Of course, various admirers—for he always had a little circle of fervent lovers of his art—used from time to time to stay in the district, so as to be near him. ... Then, too, he and I were old friends, and now that I was living in the vicinity as well, I used to see a good deal of him. Indeed I believe my chief claim to renown after I have gone, will be that my articles on Dubosque's paintings helped to place him as a great modern master: but I don't think he liked me any more for that. He could have done without any of us. Even if he had made money in his lifetime it would have meant nothing to him—but, as you know, it is his widow who reaps the benefit of the vast sums his pictures fetch to-day.

"He had married this woman a few years before he settled in the neighbourhood. Perhaps he had not known much about her (for in matters of life, as opposed to those of painting, he always shared the vagueness of the disinterested) except that she had been his mistress, could cook, and liked looking after men and things. She did not, of course, he must have realized, understand his pictures, or care for them: but then, how few people did. But if they married, she could superintend the house, and so he could paint more. ...

Pompey and Some Peaches—I

There was always so little time, it seemed to him. "Deborah was tall, large-framed, a handsome creature; about forty then, some fifteen years younger than her husband. And she could be pleasant, in a natural sort of way. But soon after their marriage, she began to change. . . . Of course, in spite of the general neglect of him, he was always the centre of interest to a chosen —or, rather choosing—few, a prince of a territory composed of princes. And, now that she met his friends as equals, she became aware of it. . . . What it was all about she could not comprehend, but of one thing she was certain: he *could* make money if he wanted. But he did *not want* to, he was obstinate, pig-headed, she called it. And then, as he was poor—at any rate poor compared with many of his friends, he should not be so wasteful. Beautiful plates of apricots and peaches in the summer, just left to rot so that he could paint them! 'Mustn't touch this' and 'Mustn't touch that!' Never even asked if she'd like to eat one. And often he wouldn't even paint them, he would just sit there staring at the fruit in a way that irritated her beyond bearing, gazing at them as though he were consuming them in a sort of silent, mystic passion of the eyes. (I have often seen him do it.) Well, why didn't he eat them? He always seemed to keep the best for painting, and when once in the morning, just before he woke, she had stolen into the studio and eaten two of the peaches on the plate, he had made a row; an awful, vulgar row, to her way of thinking.

"But she'd given him as good as she got: that was one good thing. He'd never had the rough side of her tongue before, she had always treated him different from other people. But now he was her husband, and she meant to show him, just like she had shown Jack and Andy in the old days. . . . After all, if she stayed there, hour after hour, staring at the slops or the unmade bed instead of doing the chores, how would he get on, she would like to know? . . . Of course, she was fond of him, she admitted to herself (let anyone else venture to criticize him to her), but he was silly, soft, let anyone treat him anyhow, so long as he could go on painting or staring. . . . And he hardly ever looked at *her*. She was just a fixture. If only she had been an old turnip or an apple or something, he would have sat gazing at her for hours with those love-sick eyes, she supposed. No, all he cared for was his painting; and what came of it? Never even a picture in the Academy: (they might think she knew nothing about Art, but she knew that painters ought to have pictures in the Academy). And no money. She was surprised his friends weren't ashamed of him, instead of crying and fawning round, with their 'Yes, Richard' and 'No, Richard' and 'Do you really think so, Richard?'

"As for Dubosque I imagine, from what I saw, that,

as he grew ever more used to her, he became more steadily attached to her. . . . I don't know, but I think all the same that he hated her change of voice; for, as his wife, and so the equal of his friends, she had adopted a new voice, like theirs, she thought—a new accent—as she would have said. The old rustic burr, that had been one of her chief attractions for him, had vanished, except when she was angry and momentarily reverted. I used to notice, when I was with them, how her new voice continually surprised him, in the same way as the new attitude of superiority she had developed in order to match it; the jump he gave, for instance, at her 'Gharstley Creatchah!' . . . He had a pet tortoise in the garden, a wise tortoise that loved him, and, silently and slowly plodding, never interrupted him during his painting, though it entered the studio whenever it liked. 'Pompey,' he used to call it, 'Pompey, armoured as proudly as the greatest of Roman warriors.' And in the autumn, Dubosque said, Pompey would go, just like a Roman General into winter quarters, embedding himself till the spring in a mound of dry grass and sweet herbs specially prepared for him every year in the garden.

"Dubosque loved to paint Pompey. He would gaze at the tortoise for hours, enraptured, unravelling the design of its armour, the marking and corrugation of its shell. . . . You would have thought, Deborah used to say to herself, that he was in love with it, ghastly creature! And, whenever Pompey was mentioned—and Dubosque's friends always made a point of inquiring after the tortoise—she would scream out "Gharstley Creatchah!' in her new, affected voice. . . . Waste of time, she thought, looking after it; just like it was waste of money to send her to buy those roses in York, in the middle of the winter, just because he 'wanted to paint roses,' and waste of good peaches, to leave them there, rotting on the dish!

"As her husband grew older, he seemed to her to grow more obstinate. She saw in him no longer that ardent, romantic youth of thirty years before, as she had first known him, and in whom she had in some dim, groping way divined the genius, but a tired elderly man whom it was her duty to look after, but who always tried to escape and to raise difficulties. . . . As a matter of fact, in a kind of way, perhaps she was right: as often occurs with a genius, with the passing years the fire had left him, and entered exclusively into his work. It flamed through his canvases, but no longer showed in word or look or action. He was gentle now, still without guile, and he did not want to talk much even to those who would understand what he said. He seemed to enjoy, chiefly, the company of my two daughters who were then little girls; he loved the society of children. As for Deborah he always treated her kindly, and with respect in front of his friends, however trying she might be. But he was determined not to encourage her to chatter in private about the high cost of housekeeping in this part of the country, or to complain about the tortoise, when he could be alone in his studio, either painting that old bottle he had found, and a glass and some oranges, or looking at them. . . . And why did she bother about money? she had never enjoyed *any* before she married him, even if they did not have much now.

"His health gave way before such a collapse was due or could have been foretold. The fire had burnt him up. He cannot have been more than sixty. I know that, because we were about the same age, and that was eighteen years ago. . . . I suppose to you it sounds a great age: but I can assure you, as one gets on, it seems nothing at all. . . . But to continue. . . . It was that final winter on the wolds that finished him. In the autumn, when the last flowers, belated white roses and scarlet snapdragon, still nodded in the particular misty, golden sunshine of its early mornings and late evenings, we warned him. Already he had begun to cough. His friends, my wife and myself among them, implored him to go abroad, to Italy or the South of France, for the winter. But he would not listen to us. Though the hours during which he could paint at this season were so few and fitful, this was his chosen light, the light by which he saw, in which he lived and all objects lived for him.

"Just as the painters of Italy and the Netherlands have recorded for ever the quality and texture of the days in their countries, so it has been left, it seems to me, to two English painters alone, to Constable first, and then to Dubosque, to sum up and present the look and feeling of the light of their native land. This peach or this jug could have been painted nowhere else in the world: and an apple or an egg, which to the ordinary eye has so little individuality, was to him, in this clear, pure light, more beautiful, more worthy of being looked at, examined, searched, as it were, than were the most sumptuous objects elsewhere, the great mosaics of Constantinople or the jewelled enamels of medieval France.

"It was this light which 'sang' to him. . . . But, alas, this winter, his beloved light failed him. It was not that his eyesight had begun to go, but that the light itself suffered a change, for the snow, when it first fell, did not melt in a day or two, as usual, but rolled over the abrupt and breath-taking perspective of these parts its thick ugly carpet. It was impossible for him to indulge, even, in that laziest and most agreeable winter pastime of the painter, to look at the pictures he had painted in the summer and criticize them. He could not 'see them,' he complained. (Grumbling again, Deborah

said to herself, as if no one had ever seen snow before!
. . . Why couldn't he set to work now, and make
money? . . . Portraits, for example. . . . Why, they'd
easily be in time for the Academy, if he started them
now. She saw it in her mind's eye, 'Study in Scarlet and
Silver: the Artist's Wife' . . . . And everyone stopping
before it in admiration.)

"Day after day the snow lay there, or it snowed
again: day after day in consequence lost interest for
him. There was nothing to do. Wise Pompey slept in
his mound: there was no fruit to look at, and even if
there had been, it would signify nothing. Every morning the same white light entered when he pulled the
curtains, a hard, pitiless whiteness that glared up
through the windows of the cottage from the ground,
reached the white ceiling, to fall back with a redoubled
white numbness on to the objects in the room or studio.
He could see nothing, look at nothing. He wandered
about continually, in and out of the house, wondering
when the sky would alter, and the whole world with
it. Surely it could not go on, day after day? Within
himself, he asked which of his peers in painting would
have derived inspiration from these scenes? Manet,
perhaps, would have intoxicated his senses with this
new light, and its effect on familiar things: the swooping lines of the wolds and the movement of the thick,
fore-shortened figures on the frozen mere below, would

have brought ecstasy to the heart and hand of Breughel the Elder; but to him, Dubosque, this world in which the ground in the distance was more light and perceptible, and stretched further, than the sky above, held a terrible quality of sterilization, as though the whole country had been transferred into a hospital ward.

"So he fidgeted, and grew to look more and more miserable. Deborah, who usually attacked him for working too hard, and thinking of nothing but his work, now reversed the engine, as it were, and, in the old language of her unregenerate days, 'ticked him off proper' for being lazy. Why didn't he go to sleep for the winter, and bury himself in a heap of leaves, like Pompey, 'Gharstley Creatchah'? But, even if *he* could, she couldn't afford to stand about talking all day: any more than she could afford to leave peaches about like his Lordship. (Oh no, she didn't forget those things!) *She* had work to do. She must, somehow or other, and it wasn't easy in this weather, get to the village, for shopping—otherwise he'd have nothing to eat, and how would he like that? And also to see the new boy, who was coming in, as soon as the weather altered, twice a week to help keep the garden tidy. (She didn't like his friends to go away and say she didn't know how to keep the place properly for him, even if he didn't mind!) . . . But there it was, if he went on mooning about like that, he'd catch another cold, and then she'd have to nurse him, too, she supposed.

"And catch cold, sure enough, he did. . . . By then it was February, and the cold settled on his lungs. I saw him. In the morning, Deborah said, he had been quite clear in his mind, but in the afternoon he was both listless and feverish. Deborah did not seem to think much of it: it would pass. But I was disturbed about his condition. And though I didn't like the two children to see anyone seriously ill, for they were only about fifteen and sixteen then, I told them to ride over and call on him one day soon. I knew he was particularly attached to them—and they to him—and I thought their visit would cheer him up. When they went, they took with them—dear girls, it was their own idea— a basket of South African peaches, which they had bought specially for him in York out of their own money.

"It was, apparently, a lovely afternoon that they chose for their visit, mild and full of a serene light, for at last the weather had changed, and the snow had melted. Deborah took them in to see him. 'Look, Rich, what lovely peaches they've brought you,' she said, as they entered the room. . . . But he had seemed very odd, that afternoon, hardly noticed the children, they thought, and they returned home very distressed about him. From what they said, I don't believe he recognized them at all. He mumbled something when they came in, and then his eyes followed the basket of peaches, that swam that afternoon in a perfect painter's light. His eyes devoured them, he appeared to see nothing else. . . . And then suddenly, as he remained in this rapt staring at the fruit, large tears began to roll down his finely sculptured cheeks; rolled down them. But he did not speak. . . . The children thought it better to go home: it was too painful. As they left, they heard Deborah, behind them, reproving her patient for his manners. 'That's a nice way to say "Thank you" for a present. . . . Such lovely peaches, too. I shouldn't think they'd bring you anything another time.'

"When the children told me, it sounded to me like his farewell to the visual world he had loved and served so well. . . . After that, in the next three days I can only piece together what happened, from things Deborah and the doctor told me: I did not like to go over and interfere myself, and, indeed, now that pneumonia had set in, there was nothing one could do. I am sure Deborah looked after him well in her own way. But a year or two before, when they had the quarrel about which I told you over the peaches, he had said to me, laughing—for he told me about it at the time, making a joke of it—'If ever I see her eating another of my peaches, I believe it will kill me!' And that, I believe, is, in a sense, exactly what occurred.

"He was only allowed orange juice, nothing to eat, the doctor said, when I telephoned to ask if there was any food I could send over for him. He had been told he could have a peach. But he would not; he just lay there, Deborah complained, staring at the basket, looking at the peaches with gooseberry eyes. Just the same he was, well or ill. She priced them up in her mind. They must have cost from 1s. 6d. to 1s. 9d. each, at least. And they'd been there three days, wouldn't last another twelve hours, and if there was one thing she hated, it was waste! . . . Now that it was growing too dark to go on staring at the peaches, he had shut his eyes. He must be asleep, she thought, so she snatched a peach. He wouldn't notice, was feverish all the time.

"Delicious, it was, but difficult to eat, there was so much juice in it. It ran down the corners of her chin, and she had to gobble it to prevent the juice from spoiling her dress. (There, that was better.) But just as she was finishing it, a glow shone in through the window. Something must be alight in the garden; a bonfire. It showed her face very clearly and outlined her figure against the darkness. The dying painter opened his eyes and saw her, huge and dominating, in his sick brain, against the darkness, her face, very clear, as she munched, with the little rivulets of juice wetting her chin. For a moment he sat up and watched with intensity. 'Richard, Richard!' she cried, but he had fallen back, and his panting for breath had ended.

"Outside in the garden, the bonfire began to die down. Near its still incandescent heart, Pompey, that 'Gharstley Creatchah,' 'armoured as proudly as the greatest of Roman warriors,' had been sleeping. . . . The new garden boy had forgotten, had thought the mound in which Pompey passed his royal winter sleep, was rubbish to be burned.

"Later, his gutted shell was found in the ruins of his funeral pyre. For a long time Deborah would not throw it away. After all, she said to herself, it was tortoise-shell, and might be worth something to the right person, to someone who was looking for such a thing. I believe when she left, she took it up with her to London. . . . That was eighteen years ago, or so. But it was only two years ago that she parted, for eight thousand pounds, with the famous 'Pompey and some Peaches,' which used to hang over the chimney-piece of her house in South Audley Street."

Pompey and Some Peaches—II

"Everything is the same," Miss Gertrude Stein says somewhere, "and everything is different." When the doctor told me the same story, it sounded different.

"If I were an artist feller, I wouldn't mind painting that view myself," he said to me one day, looking out of the window of the bedroom in which I lay ill. "But I'm surprised *you* never have a shot at it! I should have thought painting was in your line.—Besides, a man ought to have hobbies. You'd find your health much better if you took to one.

"You're so artistic and all that, you ought some time

when you're in London to go and call on Mrs. Dubosque. I've often wondered why you don't. She'd be pleased to see you, I know. And I'm sure the pictures would interest you: a wonderful collection. . . . Oh, my God no! *Real* pictures; not by her husband. She got rid of most of them ages back. The last went two years ago—fetched eight thousand pounds, if you please!

"Never could make out how they brought those prices. Extraordinary thing. . . . Of course, I'm only a country doctor, so I know nothing about it. I don't pretend to be a judge. But to my mind they were just daubs, anybody could have done them. (The other day, the wife showed me a drawing in coloured chalks, what they call crayons, by Elise, our little girl, and I can tell you it was a masterpiece compared to many of his things.) He just didn't know how to put the paint on. I've never seen any other painter put it on like that. Never could understand how he got it across—and yet some of the critics thought the world of him. It's my belief you or I could hoodwink them, if we wanted to. . . . Anyhow, as I was telling you, with the money she made out of the sale of his pictures, she bought a house in South Audley Street and some magnificent paintings, new, as well as old. After her husband died, she used to go round the Academy every year and pick out the best, didn't mind what she paid for 'em. Real high-class things, with no nonsense about them.

"Oh, Deborah's got taste! You can see it directly you enter the house. You'd be surprised at the dining-room, a huge great room, painted like that green stuff from Russia, with black marble pillars, and over the mantel-piece a magnificent portrait of her by Lazló. It's a stunner: real good style, in a silver dress with a tiara and white fox fur, and her pearls. (Lovely pearls, she's got.) It might be her herself—and opposite, another one, nearly as good, by Simon Elwes.

"Of course, her hair is white now (by Jove, didn't Lazló know how to paint white hair well!), but she's still a fine-looking woman. You know, one of those figures, like that," and the doctor stuck out his chest, and drew Mrs. Dubosque for me on the empty air. "Very striking, with wonderful eyes.

"I first came up to this mouldy part of the country just after I'd qualified. Knew nobody. Of course, I've got used to it, but it seemed funny then, after always living at the governor's tidy little place at Wimbledon. One was at the heart of things there, and could always run up to town for a show and supper afterwards, and get back easily. . . . So it seemed very cut-off and uncivilized here. No tennis. And I missed my people and the girls (three sisters, I had then). No one to talk to. . . . So

Open the Door!

I suppose I was rather taken by Deborah—Mrs. Dubosque—and I often used to walk up there and talk to her. In time we became very good friends, for we 'spoke the same language,' as they say.

"People used to have it that she'd been a bit gay in her time, but I never saw a sign of it. She was handsome then, very handsome, but what I liked most about her was the way she spoke. A lovely voice: *you know,* refined. Quite different to all the people round here. And much too good for *him,* in my opinion. Always thought he was a fake, with nothing to him. And *funny,* too. Often I've seen him sit for hours without speaking, just staring at something. *She* was the real thing, worth a hundred of him. . . . And if, after his death, his pictures fetched those ridiculous prices, it must have been her doing. A clever woman, with her head screwed on the right way, and always very careful, keen on her money's worth and hating waste. . . . He was a lucky man, if only he'd had the brains to realize it. You don't find many women like that nowadays.

"It used to make my blood boil, the way he treated her. . . . Of course, looking back—I suppose one gets more tolerant as one gets older—I can see that, though different from other people, he wasn't *all* bad. But, by Jove, he *was* a queer chap. Couldn't paint at all—that was obvious—and yet you'd have thought that nothing

but painting interested him. I wonder it didn't get
more on her nerves, the way he behaved. . . . You
know, all sorts of little things. . . . Often when I went
to see them, he'd fasten his eyes on one particular
thing, a basket of fruit it might be, or a bunch of
flowers, or that beastly, smelly tortoise he always had
about the place in the summer, and just stare and stare,
as if hypnotized. When she spoke to him, he'd often
make no reply, but just go on staring. And the same
with me, would hardly speak to me, didn't seem to
see me. (I tell you, I've attended cases no worse than
his—Dementia Praecox, they call it—in the County
Asylum before now.) Wouldn't answer when I tried
to be polite; but then, I'm a man, and it didn't matter.
But you can't treat a woman like that. (The governor
was always pretty strong about that sort of thing with
me, when I was a youngster, I can tell you. If any
man had dared to treat the Mater in that way, he'd
have knocked him down.) Yet, when some of his
friends came to see him from London—their gross flat-
tery of him used to make me feel sick—he'd fairly talk
his head off. All rot, of course, but still, it showed he
could make himself pleasant, if he wanted. And his
friends would repeat what he'd said, and even go on
repeating things he'd said years before, as if they were
wonderful.

"Dubosque was always painting that tortoise and

making a fuss of it. I can understand a chap making a friend of a fox-terrier or an airedale—after all, they're very *like us*—much more intelligent, I often say, than any human I know. . . . You know my dog 'Spot'? Well, often he'll bark at me for half an hour at a time, and I'll answer him. Each of us understands every word the other says. . . . But a tortoise! I wouldn't touch one with a pair of tongs. *A tortoise!* And I'm sure Deborah can't have liked the way he used to stroke it, and talk to it and stare at it, while paying no attention to her. But she never said much, not even to me. . . . Sometimes, she'd just look at it and say, in a voice that showed how much above that sort of thing she was, 'Ghastly Creature!' Just like that, 'Ghastly Creature!' Withering!

"And then he was so mean. I suppose he wasn't rich, but he didn't seem to *want* to make money. (It was as though it didn't interest him, extraordinary chap.) Still, he had a little put by: she'd seen to that. But he seemed to grudge her every single thing, even the fruit he was painting. Often I've seen him forbid her to eat a peach, or even an apple, just because he happened to be painting it. ('The poet of still life,' indeed!) No, it had to be treated like something sacred, not dusted, not touched. Sometimes—there weren't any people up there for her to talk to—she'd confide in me. And I remember her telling me that once she'd taken two peaches off a plate in the studio, because she saw they'd be bad by the next day, and had eaten them herself, so as not to feel that they'd all been wasted. But, when he noticed, he made a fearful rumpus, went right off the deep end. . . . Well, you know, it's not nice, that sort of thing. It isn't playing the game with a woman. It wasn't straight. . . . And another thing. In those days—though you wouldn't think it to look at her now—she used to do most of the housework herself, and liked sometimes to sing as she worked. But he wouldn't let her. Said it distracted him at his painting! Imagine it! . . . At the same time, nothing was good enough for that beastly tortoise. 'Pompey', as his friends used to call it, could have anything he damned well liked. Milk in saucers all over the place at all hours of the day, lettuces and fresh fruit and rose petals in the summer, and in the winter, a special mound of grass and stuff for him to sleep in, piled up for him in the garden.

"As for Dubosque, summer or winter you could hardly get him out of the house. I'm surprised his legs didn't atrophy! Never took any exercise, and when I spoke to him about it—he was my patient (we doctors can't pick and choose our patients, unfortunately; have to place our scientific knowledge at the disposal of anyone who needs it), and it was my duty to look after him, whatever I thought of his 'art'—and told him, straight out, that he must walk more and take more fresh air; what do you think he replied? . . . That he 'hadn't time'! That'll show you the sort of feller he was. Lazy as they're made. And did nothing but paint —and paint badly at that, to my mind! . . . After all, it's not a matter of argument, but of fact. What would happen to me if I diagnosed measles, and it proved to be gall-stones or appendicitis? In the same way, a peach is a delicate thing, no one can pretend it isn't, so it's obviously bad art to paint it with great, heavy, clumsy strokes. All thumbs, as you might say. (In a moment, when I've finished what I'm telling you, I'll show you a little gem of a water-colour of some peaches and a bit of mimosa that the wife did on our holiday at Cannes last spring. . . . I appreciate good work when I see it.) So it used to make me cross to hear his silly friends discussing his way of painting in their mincing, art jargon: 'Richard's brushwork is superb!' or 'Just look at the broad treatment of those roses!' or 'I feel I've never seen a tortoise before, till I looked at that picture!' Affected set of beggars, if ever there was one!

"He didn't show it much to me, but he had a *nasty* temper. Sulked about things that wouldn't affect you and me. So, one year, when the snow came down nearly every day for two months, it happened not to suit him, and he fell ill and developed 'pneumo.' After all, it's never exactly the Riviera-touch in this neighbourhood during the winter; he ought to have known that, being born up here. Besides, you'd think that any real artist would have liked the snow. Lovely, it was. But I think he'd begun to go a bit balmy as well; and 'pneumo' always attacks mentals. No resistance, you see. . . . Well, for weeks beforehand, he'd been skulking about the house and garden, sulking, and now, when he fell ill, he'd hardly speak; hardly even speak to me, though I was his medical adviser. Deborah behaved like an angel, the way she nursed her husband: and all the pipes bursting from the frost, all over the place; worked her fingers to the bone for him. He never so much as said 'Thank you,' just lay there, in bed, and even when the weather changed and became mild, he didn't get any better. Made no effort. And no doctor can cure a patient unless he tries to cure himself.

"Then one afternoon, some friends of his—the daughters of 'Old Maure,' as they call him here, affected old blighter—brought him a basket of peaches. Very kind of the children, really, don't you know. Had paid for them themselves. But when he saw the fruit, he paid no attention to anyone or anything else, but began to blubber, without even speaking to the little things who'd brought it; there he lay for hours, tears running down his face, and staring at the peaches—which, I must say, looked very good—in a way that made one's blood curdle. . . . Perhaps he knew he wouldn't see any fruit where he was going. But he should have been more considerate to his wife, and not shown his feelings. Besides, they'd been got for him to eat. (I allowed him fruit and things like that and orange juice: one day when we've got more time, I'll give you my views on orange juice.) But he wouldn't touch them. Just left them there in the basket, and stared, and stared, perverse devil that he was.

"There the peaches stayed, on a table by his bed for two or three days. I went back to visit him one day in the evening; when I entered the room, it was difficult to see at first, it was dark, but there was a sort of glow coming through the window. The patient was lying back, asleep,—a good sign, for he'd been very restless— and Deborah was standing in the middle of the room. I'd walked up the stairs quietly, and she didn't see me, and, I don't know why, but I stood still in the doorway. There seemed something important, dramatic's the word, about it. There she stood, you know, a great, big woman, outlined by that funny sort of light. 'Eerie,' I suppose, people would call it. I remember thinking how fine she looked, monumental. The windows were opposite, and this queer red glow wavered round her body, and shone full on her face. She was eating one of the peaches, because he wouldn't eat them, and they'd have gone bad by the next day. But what struck me was, I'd never seen anyone enjoy anything so much as she enjoyed that peach. It did one good to watch her (that's what I admired about her, the way she made you feel she'd enjoy things), and you could see it was a lovely, juicy peach. . . . At that very moment he sat up in bed, suddenly, without warning. And there was just enough light to see him staring and staring at Deborah, without saying a word. When she saw him, for at first she was intent on the peach, I could see it gave her a fright, for she uttered a cry. Then he fell back, still without saying a word.

"I had to sign the death certificate. I very nearly entered 'Temper' as the cause of death: for that is what it was, in my humble opinion. Sheer rage, because she was eating one of his peaches. Real dog-in-the-manger: wouldn't eat it himself, and wouldn't let anyone else eat it. Much rather it went bad. . . . Now can you imagine a man's mind working like that? Extraordinary. Just Temper. . . . But, of course, he'd undermined his constitution, too, by never going out and by working at all sorts of hours.

"And, do you know, that tortoise died at the same time? A new garden lad mistook the creature's mound for a rubbish-heap, and had set a light to it. And that's what the glow came from, in the room. . . . Of course, Dubosque didn't know that, or he'd have died twice over from rage. . . . Funny thing," he added, rising unexpectedly to a point of imagination, "the way those two died together, like a witch and what they used to call . . . what was it? . . . a familiar spirit.

"Then, after he was dead, the dealers and critics set to, to their games and, between them, rushed the prices up. . . . And Deborah, I must say, got out while the going was good, though,—the most odd thing of all —the prices, I'm told, are higher than ever. . . . But I always say, it can't last. After all, it's people like you and me who are the final judges. . . . And I wouldn't pay a penny, not for one of them. . . . Anyhow, she's made good; she's a rich woman. *And* charitable! Always doing her bit at those balls and supper parties and things you read about in the papers. . . . Sometimes I wish I'd had more time for painting, myself."

The Woman Who Hated Flowers

My parents had sent me into a nursing-home. The hours were of the usual grey monotony, and the day nurses seemed to spend their periods of duty in whisking flowers in and out of the room, pouring more water into the vases or spilling a little out of them, in offering me glasses of a thick, viscous barley-water, very tainted in its taste, and in talking interminably—it was spring—about "daffies."

The night nurse, though, in spite of her plainness, was not ordinary; in her quietness, she was unusual. Her voice was a human voice, containing no special inflections for the "cheering up" of patients. She brought into the room a certain air of humanity, a quality of comfort. Reserved, placid, her lashless eyes—the irises, not the whites—shone sometimes with a glow of their own, as she sat gazing absorbedly into the embers, while her tall, spare body rocked a little, and by this movement rescued itself from the immobility of sculptured stone.

One night, I believe she told me her story. . . . But I could never be quite sure, for every evening I became feverish, and she never referred to the incident afterward.

When she came in, the day nurse had only just left me and had omitted to turn down the lights. I saw the newcomer breathe heavily as she entered, her nostrils dilating. Then, their scent attracting her attention, she noticed a vase of flowers—wallflowers, they were—which her predecessor had forgotten to remove, and at once carried it away into the passage.

This action I thought out of keeping with her usual dignity and slow-moving restraint, just like that of any other nurse. . . . On her return, she stood watching me for several minutes without speaking, then said, suddenly, with great force, "I *hate* flowers," switched off the lights and went out.

I woke up later, and could distinguish her figure by the fire. She was rocking a little, as though her body were still seeking that marvellous balance which her soul at such cost, and with so little reason, had long

The Woman Who Hated Flowers

found. Sleepily I asked her, speaking partly to myself, "Why do you hate flowers?" And perhaps the fact that I was then very young, or perhaps merely the anonymity of darkness, made her tell me. But alas, from this distance I can no longer offer you her precise words, can only tell you what I remember.

Aurelia Graybourne had come out of a comfortable home in the suburbs of Dublin, but it nevertheless contained a spiritual suffering that outweighed material circumstances. Her father had long been dead, her three sisters were married, and her mother drank with ardour and endurance, devoting her life to this almost touching appetite. For its sake, she would brook any discomfort, mental, physical or of the soul. Even the priests proved unable to restrain her in her pursuit of it.

The outward respectability of Aurelia's middle-class home, the chintzes, the bureaus, the fringed cushions, the calendars, the "easy-chairs," the "occasional tables," the Victorian knickknacks in silver, all threw into a greater relief the grotesque horror of life within its walls. Hogarth's "Gin Alley" would have supplied a far more apposite background for the squalor of dozens of empty whisky bottles, ingeniously but often inadequately concealed, and for this snoring torpor or crazy gaiety that resulted from them. The working-up of scenes, the horrid, dull satisfaction of the drunkard in the pain which her inspired words could give and the subsequent maudlin scenes of reconciliation, poisoned equally the whole existence of this young girl.

Even when drunk, Mrs. Graybourne, as the daughter of one officer and the widow of another, felt obliged to keep up appearances, so she sought no convivial cronies but vented all the technique of her recurring bouts upon her youngest daughter. In the morning, when well enough, she went out shopping alone, a sort of martyred, mystical sweetness, together with a very red nose, being the only visible tokens of those hectic afternoons and evenings which she spent in the torture, conscious and unconscious, of the being most dear to her in the world.

Eventually, after a very bad outbreak, the doctors and priests intervened and insisted on the eldest daughter, now a widow herself, coming to look after Mrs. Graybourne. They said she needed someone of experience with her. . . . During this interlude, Aurelia declared her intention of entering a convent. Ada, her sister, who, though perfectly aware of what had been going on, had, until the priests sent for her, never offered to help in any manner, now took sides openly against her. But Aurelia was just of age, and could do what she liked: (she possessed a hundred and fifty pounds a year of her own). No one could move her, hitherto so gentle.

Mrs. Graybourne, too ill to argue, wept a great deal,

The Woman Who Hated Flowers

but could not succeed in persuading Aurelia to remain at home. At last, though, she relented sufficiently to promise that for the first two or three years she would work as a lay sister, thus giving herself time to see whether she was fitted for the novitiate. But this affectation of lowliness, as she chose to consider it, yet further embittered the convalescent.

When Aurelia left, Mrs. Graybourne was still confined to her bed. Sweetness and resignation, with a dash of menace and a hint of prophecy, were her specialities at the moment.

"To think that you should leave a loving mother and a comfortable home, all because of your own unnatural selfishness," she had begun, when the cab was at the door. But sobs choked her at this point, and she had been obliged to pause. "I've nothing to say against convents," she had continued, in her wily brogue. "I'm a religious woman, I hope. But I warned Father Clement . . . 'That girl will bring disgrace on St. Ursula's, just as she has on her poor mother.'"

Aurelia had driven up to the convent in an old cab, through pouring rain, but in spite of the clouds that lay low upon the mountains, her heart was at rest. From the first moment when the Abbess received her, she felt she had done the only thing that could give her peace. The rain, the calm, the routine, soothed her nerves and made her happy. Through serving so humbly, she regarded herself already as dedicated to God's service. Perhaps Mrs. Graybourne's reproaches had touched her, and underneath her extreme devoutness may have existed the apprehension that only by an entire surrender of herself could she atone for abandoning the earthly ties of duty, however degrading and destructive. Henceforth no task could be too menial for her.

The severity of the life suited her. Her eyes took on reflections of sea and lake and cloud and mountain, and her skin attained the delicate suffusion of colour that tinges Irish cheeks alone, nourished by generations of soft, continual rain. Notwithstanding her desire for self-suppression, a sort of animal radiance, derived from a new contentment with her surroundings, became manifest in her, showed through the movements of her limbs, encumbered by their heavy, medieval, garment, and, with the conviction it carried of youth and innocence, appealed to every heart.

The seasons were quickened in their passing by the regular tenor of her existence. Twice she had seen the winter disappear. Soon she would become a novice, and sever the last tie with her old self. Meanwhile a thousand tasks employed her time, cleaning the rooms and passages, gentle gardening, picking fruit. Since she had soon won the trust and affection of the nuns, she would often be left alone at such pursuits. Or it would be her duty to sweep out and adorn the chapel; that Irish-Gothic edifice of the nineteenth century, vast and ill-proportioned, every pillar and arch too narrow and too poor, but built, nevertheless, with a sense of the theatre, full of bright light and deep shadow and incense through which the realistically painted saints trailed flaring and tawdry dresses, their shrines decorated with arrangements of tinsel and imitation flowers.

Outside now, the days of spring were thick and heavy with a pagan, impermanent joy. The sunlight issued in spears and shafts from behind fat, lolling clouds. It lay like cream upon clustered blossom of apple and pear tree, and gilded with a warm effulgence the grass at their roots, throwing into vivid individual relief the flowers among it. The wallflowers, with their turrets of crumpled tawny velvet, growing by the base of the chapel walls, hummed with drowsy insect life, and their sweetness, which appeared to be less a scent than the very perfume of the golden day itself, hung above the paths and entered a little way into the chapel, there to be defeated by the Christian smell of incense. Often, the glittering lances of the showers, in their sudden charges, similarly dispersed it for a time in the garden itself. . . . But directly the sun came through, those sweet odours mounted once more into the air. Vague, luxuriant longings of the flesh assailed her, and she would return to the chapel for the seeming permanence of its meagre arch and pillar, cold stone and hard benches, to allay them. These by now familiar objects offered their own assurance; here things were as they always were, had been, would be, unaltered and inalterable as the love of God. The life in the garden, though temporarily disturbing to the senses, was fitful, seasonal. . . . But how sinful, she reflected, that the flesh of men and women should be subject to these earthy and godless permutations.

Nevertheless, as she swept clear of dust the ugly ecclesiastical patterns of the tessellated floor with her medieval broom—composed, like a gardener's, of twigs bound together—she was conscious that the joy from outside had invaded the most sacred places. The welling up of life in her body, as much as in every tree and flower, now tinctured for her every inanimate object, so that paper flowers appeared to blossom more bravely, the patterned floor to assume harder, brighter colours, the incense, even, to become less spiritual in its appeal.

One day, when she was sweeping the chapel, she thought she would look into the street and, just as she opened the door, it happened that a man she had known in Dublin passed by. About ten years older than herself, he was a musician (indeed, many thought that he possessed great talent as a composer), and her mother disapproved of him, which had added to his already considerable charm. In spite of the change in her attire, he recognized her at once. (She supposed, afterwards, that, when he called her name, she ought not to have answered; but how could she have refused, it would have been rude and unkind?) She stood there in the warm shadow, and he, in full sunlight, so that it beat down on his dark, handsome face and bold jutting features, and showed her a flattering admiration, surprise and pleasure in his large, dark eyes, usually nonchalant and melancholy. As he spoke to her, her whole body came to life beneath the heavy, stone-like folds of her dress, as though a statue were starting to breathe.

After that, she did not so clearly remember the course of events. Some intoxication of the senses appeared to have affected her, leaving behind it a state bordering on oblivion. For about two months, however, she struggled for her beliefs; then she began to meet Terence Marlowe by appointment on many occasions. After all, she would argue with herself, she was free, she had as yet taken no vows.

Chance favoured their love for each other; almost miraculously, they were never seen together. The months passed. But though gay and happy when in his company, at other times a consciousness of the wickedness of what he had asked her—and what she intended —to do, weighed her down. For he pleaded with her continually to abandon the idea of the cloister and run away to London; where, later, he would come to marry her. . . . Not at once, or the Abbess and the nuns would talk, and would no doubt find a way of injuring him in the eyes of members of his family. And that, neither he nor Aurelia could afford, because by copying out parts and by playing the organ, he was earning little enough money: but he possessed expectations of a moderate sort from his relatives.

Many were the nights when desolation of the spirit kept her awake, and by day in the garden, as she swept the paths and inhaled the perfume of the wallflowers, her face often burned with shame. But at other moments, when she reflected that Terence loved her, just as she loved him, a certain feeling of joy and pride comforted her. . . . It was indeed fortunate, she would then reflect, that she had allowed her family to persuade her to wait, before making any irrevocable decision. She could still escape. The life of the convent would soon be behind her, just as was the life of her old home. . . . Almost she had forgotten the existence of her mother and sister, the protests and uproar that would arise when they heard that she was taking their advice. . . . Meanwhile, she could not bring herself to tell the Abbess or consult the nuns, though, but for her fear, there was nothing to prevent her. No obstacles would have been placed in her way, whatever she decided to do. . . . But in her own mind, she still regarded herself as dedicated to the service of God, not of man.

The Woman Who Hated Flowers

. . . She loved them, so she must run away without saying good-bye.

When she ran away, leaving behind her a letter to the Abbess, worded in a business-like, brisk manner, she hardly experienced the remorse she had anticipated. It seemed no more than the changing of her old-fashioned livery for dress of the times. In the same style, her old life was folded up, hidden out of sight. She stood on deck now—so she felt—a modern figure, finished with restraints, welcoming the life of the day. And though numbered among those in whose hearts, however much they may transgress its teachings, religion had taken root, and would never die, of this she was unconscious, and rejoiced as the sea and air sang the word "freedom" in her ears.

She was to wait a month in London for her lover. At first time sped by, but, as day followed day and six weeks and more had elapsed, it began to drag. His early letters, long and affectionate, had been frequent as even she could wish, but they were now few. And, although living cheaply in a boarding-house in Blooms-bury, her money showed signs of becoming exhausted. She began to lose interest in this city, so new to her. . . . And still he did not arrive to claim her. . . . Not even now, however, not for a moment, did she doubt him. If she did, the world would fall in ruins round her.

Open the Door!

Letters began to arrive from her mother and sisters, who had succeeded at last in tracing her. These contained dull reproaches, coarse taunts and much talk of the suffering she had brought upon them. "You have," Mrs. Graybourne wrote, "cast a slur upon your own father's good name." ... *Who* was the *man?* the chorus demanded and reiterated. ... Aurelia did not answer. ... Then Ada came to see her, and talked of their mother as a martyr, never even allowed herself to admit that Mrs. Graybourne drank. *Who was the man?*

All right, if she would not say, they would find out. But, whoever he might be, he was after her fortune. (To many men, it might seem a lot.) Of that, both Ada and Mrs. Graybourne were sure.

At last a letter arrived. It could not have been an easy letter to write. ... She opened it in her room. He was afraid, he said, that she might think he had been silly, but he was sure that if they had gone on, they would only have regretted it. He had just married; an old friend of his. He hoped Aurelia would be sensible and would not write to him, as Elise might see the letter and it would upset her, since she knew nothing about their friendship. ...

So they were wrong! He was not after her money; nor after herself. It had been merely a matter of play. ... He had waited two months—until the spring had come again—and then had married this woman of whom she had never heard.

"Nothing," that was the word that haunted Aurelia. Nothing. It had meant nothing: nothing. She was not even to be given the crown of a great betrayal. It was all paltry, insignificant. She felt sick, suddenly, as though she were going to die. (She could not bear that scent of wallflowers: on her dressing-table stood a small bunch she had bought yesterday. She got up, took it from the vase, went to the window, and threw it out into the yard.) Nothing. . . . For days she stayed in her room, shunning the light, sitting dully in her chair in her sordid, damp-stained attic, for she feared the repercussion, even from a distance in a great city, of the humming ecstasy of apple trees in flower and the indefinable, pervading sweetness of wallflowers. She feared the air itself.

At any rate this intolerable misery had been real. Soon—after the passage of these first few days, and then of a month or two—she was real no longer, even to herself: nothing. Now she could go out again, buy newspapers, walk in parks, reply to letters; reply to them, moreover, hit by hit, kick below the belt by answering kick. But she was nothing.

Her religion, dormant in her, proved of no avail, for she had betrayed it, as Terence had betrayed her. She could not face a confessor. . . . To what could she turn, so as to escape the misery of the senses, to avoid trees and music, sunlight and moonlight and, above all, flowers?

She found the answer. Hospitals resembled convents in their routine; only the religious core was absent. She was intelligent and soon learnt her profession. And in this world of order, devoted to healing the body, she found an anodyne for her wounded soul. Its matter-of-factness, its strict rules, its divisions of light and darkness, were helpful to her, and the antiseptic smell of ward and corridor drove out the scent of the day and season, triumphed over the perfume of the flowers in the wards, sterilized them.

It was she thought, as though her heart had been cauterized. She altered in her aspect, became part of the hospital and its routine. Her body now seemed rhythmless and without purpose, except for giving medicines and smoothing pillows. Her efficiency transcended kindness, a loveless, sublimated love. And, if she felt no pleasure, she felt no pain. . . . Night-duty she enjoyed, for then she saw no daylight, slept through it and the flowers had been put away by the time she arrived in the evening.

For many years (endless years, they appeared to her) this kind of existence continued; until you would have thought that Fate had forgotten her, had thrown her life aside, intending to make no pattern out of it. . . . And then, one night, a case was brought into her ward, a drunken man, who had been knocked down and crushed by a motor-car. . . . She recognized him at once. He had become poor and old, his talent for music had come to nothing. His wife had left him. He had no children. . . . There was no one to look after him except Nurse Aurelia.

She used to sit with him in the daytime, as well as nurse him at night. The great bare windows were flooded with the golden light of unforgettable spring days, and the scent of the flowers that had been brought to the patients by relatives and friends, apple blossom and cherry, tulips, narcissus and wallflower, was often overpowering under the strong sun. . . . Day by day the old man grew worse, and after ten days he died. He had never been fully conscious, so she was not sure how much he knew or whether he recognized her. . . . But somehow or other, through looking after him, she had regained her faith.

After it was all over, she had left the hospital and taken a post in a nursing-home. She had felt she needed a change, she said.

Nurse Aurelia was silent for a while, staring into the embers, and then she turned to me, the irises of her eyes glowing with that strange fire of the animal world, and added, "But I still hate flowers."

The Messenger

It was in the afternoon, for there were no evening performances. We had both of us seen *Les Sylphides* a hundred times, and much better danced, so we left the theatre and waited in the empty *foyer* until the next ballet began.

Painters are apt to talk well: writers, badly; for by the end of the day they are tired of words. (The members of no other profession are obliged to express themselves solely by means of their wares.) Robert Lorrinder, though an excellent writer—no less original and celebrated as an author than his wife is as a painter—stands out as an exception to this rule. I love to listen to him, however preposterous may be the theories which he continually expounds, for underneath the queer brand of decorative nonsense in which invariably he indulges, gleams a vein of truth; a vein strange and at first unconvincing, because so unlike the truth of other people.

A man passed, without seeing us, and Robert smiled, and called out to him, "Good luck!"

"That's my mascot," he remarked to me. "And he knows it. I feel elated, for whenever good fortune is in the wind for me, I see him—though I have never got to know him very well. But he understands that, too. It's part of his contract, so to speak."

"If you both like the Ballet, it's inevitable that you should see him," I began to argue. "I don't think much of your reasoning, Robert."

" 'Inevitable,' *inevitable*," he repeated, "don't use that word, *please*. . . . Did I tell you about The Messenger? . . . No? Then I must tell you now. . . . 'Inevitable' is the word I dread. All my life I have been able to hear the Juggernaut creaking down the immutable course of its steel rails towards its destiny. I cannot explain the reason *why* things happen as they do; I can only humbly note fragments of the design, the vast scale of its conception, here and there the minute working out of the details attached to it. . . . You know that I have long held that, if you are frightened of something happening, that event is brought so much the nearer to you by your fear: or you may even be treated to a counterfeit semblance of it or a rehearsal for it, in order further to terrify you. The sort of thing I mean is that, if you have peculiar dread of, shall we say, smallpox, and think you have been exposed to infection, then, the very day on which you expect to develop the disease, your body will come out in a rash: but, instead of smallpox, it will prove to be some lesser, children's illness. . . . But I mustn't wander away from the question of inevitability.

"You know that I believe, too, that we are born into the world with certain people for our companions; these alone we may see, play with, quarrel with: you cannot avoid them. We are confined with them, as it were, in a compartment of eternity of which the walls are invisible, so as to give us the illusion of the whole earth at our choice. It is futile to try to escape the reiterant impacts of these people on our lives. They may bore us, they may enchant us, but there, sure enough, they will stand at our life's end as at our life's beginning. . . . And this story—an episode more than a story—which I want to tell you, shows at least how superb is the timing of Destiny, and proves that it is of no use attempting to delay the effects she wishes to obtain.

"First of all, let us for a moment examine the nature of the playmates provided for us. I hope I am not over-superstitious, but I observe coincidences. . . . There is the man who passed by just now, for instance; my mascot. Obversely, there are those whose presence darkens the air for me, the harbingers of evil. This whole genus, an important one, can be divided, I think, into two species; the first, harmless chatterers who, as the whole world reels for you though you must not show it, rush up to worry you about things that do not matter. They seem to emerge suddenly, from nowhere, with a certainty of technique that belongs only to the virtuoso—for their mere appearance discloses whole avenues leading back into the past down which Disaster stalks toward you. They like to ask questions: 'How is your dear Aunt Emily; have you heard from her lately?' or 'Did you ever get the address of that shop I wanted you to go to: you never let me know?' or 'I thought of going down to Dorset in April to stay with your cousins; will you be there?' or 'Have you seen Dicky lately?' (a man you have been avoiding for years). Indeed, this branch of the tribe never fails to collect the friends you have shed in the course of a lifetime. (And, let us be frank, the friends we possessed at eighteen are not, if we develop normally, those we should choose, or choose to see, at forty.) They are like retrievers, producing corpses for you, with an air of pride, just at the moment you least expect it. They specialize also in knowing, never the celebrated man himself, but always his duller connexions; had they then been alive, they would have concentrated their attention upon Leonardo da Vinci's maiden aunt or Michelangelo's cousin ('So much more original, yet simple,' they would have, no doubt, explained), though sometimes, no doubt, they would have materialized in some moment of agony, to ask the Master after the tedious relatives whom he had for so long striven to forget.

"The second species, however, is more incisive in action. Retrievers, too, to a man, they are also essentially the bearers of tidings. If there is something it would be better for you *not* to know at a particular moment, they spring out of the earth, like a Jinni out of his bottle, to tell you, with a grisly savouring of their pleasure, rolling the words round in their mouths in the same way that a connoisseur allows the flavour of good wine to linger upon the palate. They belong to a race apart, the witless avengers of forgotten injuries; their whole bearing, inspired by their subconscious minds, testifies to it. The countless indignities inflicted unaware upon the dwarf by the man of ordinary stature, upon the ugly by the beautiful, the stupid by the clever, boil up suddenly within their brooding blood.

"You may think I exaggerate; but let me tell you. Have patience.... Do you know Ralph Undey-Mulhall? Well, he has the attributes of both the species I have described. Please don't mistake me. He is kind—more than kind, tender-hearted. He possesses many invaluable qualities that in someone else we should all of us estimate at their true worth. He works hard, supports several idle relatives, is a faithful friend, and does good in many directions. I could never dislike him, never be rude to him. I wish him well, infinitely well, but from a distance—it must be from a distance. . . . To begin with, when I meet him he always talks to me, immediately, of those friends of my parents whom I most dislike. They speak of me, he tells me, continually, and he repeats some of 'the nice things they say.' Thus his conversation, always bringing with it the memory of distant but unhappy days, lowers the temperature of mind and heart and body. 'You cannot escape us,' the voices of the Gorgon sisters moan in your ear.

"Both Frida and I have known Ralph since we were children—before we had ever met each other. He had attended all the same children's parties to which we went. And then, when we had grown up and frequented ballrooms, there, too, he would be; now a very tall, stooping, lanky figure, dark, with a bumpy forehead, a small, clipped moustache, and brown eyes, intent but curiously empty, and a voice, deep and deliberate, summoned up like the voice of a ventriloquist rather than seeming a natural mode of expression. On these occasions he would appear always to be rather lonely, would dance seldom, so that one wondered why he came. But to us he was very friendly, and, at the time that Frida and I became engaged, just before and just after, he would invariably suggest joining us for supper. It was difficult to refuse, but you know, when you are in love, you want to be alone and don't relish extraneous company; so that, though we still liked him, we tended to try and escape his presence, but that only added, you would have thought from the result, to the fascination we exercised upon him. He was willing—and able—to ferret us out anywhere.

"The years went by then, and we saw less of him, because, as he grew older, his utter contentment, the fact that he was so happy with the collection of old silver and of our old-style-calendar friends that he was forming—for this, too, had become really a collection —irked us. He was quite rich; so, feeling the necessity of perpetuating his likeness, he sat, of course, to Lazló, and it was very trying to be invited to see that painter's flashy misrepresentation of him as a dashing Magyar magnate, rather than a mild English business-man. We grew tired of hearing of his garden, the new kind of sweet peas he was growing, and the perfection, altogether of his way of life. In fact, he was so enchanted with himself—in a lesser degree often a delightful characteristic—that it became a bore, as did his quirks and quips, his little jokes and sallies and imitations. Much more full of talk than formerly, he liked to tell you all about himself, what he ate every day, what he felt, at what time he was called and when he went to bed: these things were all of intense concern to him and so he thought they would equally interest his listeners. And he would give us, too, the opinions of his friends on many matters; he seemed to live in a perpetual house-party of those who had been dead to us since we had reached years of discretion. While, therefore, he has no spite in his whole composition, not a grain of it, he is himself its blind and unavowed instrument, the Mercury of the forces that govern the lower regions.

"You can understand how bad the last few weeks have been for us, for you know the circumstances; cruel for Frida and bad enough for me. John is our only child, and it would have been dreadful to see any child, even if he had not been our own, suffering like that, so ill and helpless and unable to understand what was the matter or tell us what he felt. And, in order to be near the right doctors, we had to stay in London through the bombing, exposing him to dangers of that kind as well.

"As a mother, Frida is sometimes a bit vague. She has always adored John, but, all the same, her whole life goes usually into her painting. (And, what's curious, I believe the little chap comprehends it and isn't jealous.) But, when he fell ill, the full strength and resilience of her character came out. She gave up her work entirely, and nursed the boy night and day. I don't know how she did it, for she wasn't used to that kind of fatigue: but I think that was what pulled him round; because it's a rare illness, and the doctors cannot help much as yet, though they do their best. For five or six weeks, she never had a thought for anyone but John. I was completely forgotten. She would hardly even allow her sister, Isabelle, to help her. The strain must have been—and anybody could see it was—immense. . . . At last, one morning, about a fortnight ago, the specialist pronounced, 'If the child gets through the next twenty-four hours, his temperature will drop. He will live, and the illness will leave no mark on him. . . . It is a terrible thing to have to say to his father and mother, but I must warn you; it all depends on the next twenty-four hours.'

"Isabelle had been splendid. Her kindness and tirelessness, her support of Frida, and the consideration she showed for her in everything, great or small, won my affection more than ever. (And I've always said that I would have married her, if I hadn't married Frida.) On the morning that the crisis of John's illness began, she came to me and said:

" 'Robert, what are we to do? . . . Natasha Danbury

is dead. She has died of pneumonia after influenza. We *can't* tell Frida at a time like this. And if we don't, she is sure to find out.'

"Natasha—I don't believe you ever met her—had been an old neighbour of Frida's parents in the country, and Frida and she had soon become great friends. As her Christian name tells you, she was Russian by origin, and she had married a delightful old man, much older than herself, Bill Danbury. He was rather an extraordinary character in his way, a squire, devoted to country pursuits, but loving books and music as much as hunting. Really, very exceptional. Natasha was beautiful, like a greyhound and, while Bill was alive, passed for an intelligent woman. Alas, when she became a widow, the full extent of the influence her husband had exercised upon her became apparent. She had absorbed his taste. But now she showed that she had no opinions of her own, though she produced every *cliché* with an impressive manner. She needed someone like Bill to grow round, and to take her out of herself. Now that he was no longer there, she brooded in a mystical way upon the intricacies of her own uninteresting nature, and expatiated upon them incessantly to her friends, in a special voice she reserved for this subject, slow and emphatic. The high points she marked, sometimes by affected spirals of laughter, sometimes by a trick she thought attractive, of putting out her tongue at right angles, and in the opposite direction from that in which she rolled her eyes. (A very difficult feat of facial acrobatics; you try it in front of the mirror when you get home!) . . . Poor Natasha! She expected her friends to give the whole of their time up to her. In the end, a year or two ago, Frida, who has all the hardness, as well as all the softness, of the artist, came to me and said:

" 'Robert, I've got to choose between Natasha and my painting. I've chosen my painting. I am fond of her, but she's inflated herself into a whole-time job, and I can't take it on. . . . Besides, she has plenty of other more suitable friends. I know she'll *pretend* to mind my neglect of her. I feel a brute, myself. But she won't *really* mind, though she will enjoy being huffy and mysterious when my name is mentioned. She won't *really* mind, because she knows how interesting her character is, how important to the world, and she knows, too, that we don't know it.'

"I don't blame Frida. Her first duty was to her painting. All the same, since she is genuinely kind, I thought I saw, from time to time, signs that Natasha weighed on her conscience. And so now the news of her sudden death—Natasha who was so healthy and had never been known to be ill for a day—was bound, especially in the circumstances in which we found ourselves, to upset Frida beyond reason.

"Her sister and I talked it over. We settled to keep *The Times* away from her—Natasha's death wasn't in the other papers—at least until our own crisis was over. If the boy took a turn for the better, she would be more fitted to hear the news; if he grew worse, nothing would matter any more. . . . The hours dragged on, the strain increasing all the time. How we got through that day and night, I shall never know. They seemed interminable. . . . Then, all at once, about eleven o'clock the next morning, the danger was over,—John's temperature had fallen, and he breathed without difficulty and slept, for the first time for a month, the easy, unstirring sleep of childhood. . . . The change was incredible at first.

"It was only, though, in this moment of utter relief, that the full fatigue of what we had been through settled upon Frida, Isabelle and myself. You can't imagine how tired we felt.

"None of us had left the house for many days, none of us had eaten a proper meal, or felt that we could eat it, and now, in spite of our exhaustion, there suddenly welled up in us a sense of gaiety, a need for relaxation. It was as though we had been on a long and very rough ocean voyage, and had at last reached land. There was no reason to stay at home any longer; John could be safely left to the nurse's care. So we decided to dine out, tired or not; but, since we did not feel inclined as yet to face people who had not shared our experience, we selected Le Perroquet Vert; because it's amusing, the food is excellent and you never see anyone you know there. . . . And since Frida still had not looked at the paper and was in this mood, we determined again to put off telling her about Natasha, to leave it to the next day; otherwise, it would only spoil her evening.

"We had ordered a table, but when we arrived, we found the *maître d'hôtel* had made a mistake, and that it had been set for four persons; a nice table with a wall-sofa and two chairs. . . . It really was enjoyable to be out of the house again, to be able to order a dinner, to be able to eat it. And there was no *alert* to-night, none of those wailings which are the signature-tune of the twentieth century. . . . We might as well have a cocktail, we thought; it was an occasion.

"Indeed, we were feeling care-free in spite of the war —and I believe both Isabelle and I had, for the time being, completely forgotten about the death of Natasha, which had been haunting us all day, because of its possible effect upon Frida.

" 'How lovely,' Isabelle said, 'to be by ourselves, but to have the whole evening before us without anything on our minds. . . . I long to hear you talk again about other things than medicines.'

"Almost as she said the words, we saw Ralph Undey-

Mulhall, sitting there, alone, in the middle of the restaurant, reading a book.

" 'It's all right, he doesn't see us,' Frida reassured us. 'And it's a good thing. I'm happy, but I'm too tired to deal with people—especially Ralph. I only want to see you two.'

" 'Oh, he sees us; never you fear.' I replied, 'He is preparing something, an eclectic joke of some kind or other, I should say.' I could deduce it from the manner in which his head never moved from behind his book.

"Isabelle urged, 'Have the fourth place removed at once! Or he'll come and sit through dinner, this heavenly sense of being at peace will be broken and we shall none of us be able to talk at all. . . . And I have masses to say; I don't know if you have? *Please* call the waiter and have it taken away.'

" 'We can't,' I said, 'it will take too long and look too rude.'

"Now a waiter hurried up to us, with a note written in pencil: 'Herr Hitler would like to look at you.' The waiter pointed out the table (we pretended not to know it), and we gazed across. Suddenly Ralph dropped his book. Then he pulled—for imitations of Hitler were fashionable at the moment, and Charlie Chaplin's 'Great Dictator' was the popular film of the hour—a lock of hair over his bumpy forehead and treated us to an impersonation of the Nazi Leader. I must say, with the

hair and his little moustache, he succeeded in looking
—though one would never have expected it—terrify-
ingly like him, or, at any rate, like other imitations of
him one had seen. . . . We smiled and laughed, in what
we hoped was a convincing manner, although the as-
tonished expression on the faces of the people sitting
at tables between us and him made us feel a little self-
conscious.

"Ralph then reassembled his features, laughed a good
deal at the joke, as he considered it, that he had played
on us, and got up and stalked toward us, rather like,
I thought, a walking lighthouse, with his lanky form and
projecting eyes, shallow but burning. He still laughed
and chuckled as he approached us. Once near enough
to speak, however, his expression changed to one of
sympathy and commiseration. . . . For an instant, I
thought he had heard, somehow or other, about John's
illness. Then I realized.

" 'Frida, dear Frida,' he was saying, 'I was *so* grieved
to hear of Natasha Danbury's death. I know what
friends you two were. Though I never knew her very
well, I had seen more of her lately, and had grown to
appreciate her, and her wonderful powers of introspec-
tion and self-analysis. Introspective people *are* so interesting, don't you think? I can quite see why you two
got on so well.'

Open the Door!

"Two spots of colour leapt suddenly into Frida's pale, tired face, and she said:

"'*Natasha? Natasha dead?* . . . Surely not? We should have heard,' and she gazed at her sister and myself with a sort of shocked inquiry and reproach in her eyes.

"There was no help for it. We had to explain.

"'Frida and I decided it was better not to tell you, darling, at present: you've had so much worry lately. We were going to break it to you to-morrow. . . . She died two days ago.' And to Ralph I said, 'You see, Ralph, I didn't let her know, because she has been nursing our little boy—and it's been a great strain. He has been very ill for weeks. But the crisis is over now. . . . This is the first time we've been out for a month: and I didn't think we should see anyone who would be likely to tell her.' . . . Meanwhile, Frida was mastering her surprise and shock.

"Ralph is kind, really very kind. An agonized look came over his face. 'Oh, how dreadful! I am so sorry. You *didn't know?* How stupid of me. I wouldn't have done such a thing for the world.'

"Then he stopped apologizing. I saw the thought go through his head, 'I must help them,' and he said, in his ordinary, deliberate way:

"'Well, as it's your first evening out, you'll want cheering up, so let *me* sit down here and talk to you.'

The Messenger

"All through our dinner—for he had finished his—
he sat in the fourth place at the table, thereby in his
own mind atoning for his lapse by charity—I never
saw a man work so hard, either, to be kind. . . . At
first, to distract Frida's attention, he talked of friends,
old friends, friends of her parents, all of them longing
to see us, he said, and often wondering how it was they
never ran across either of us. Of course, they didn't
approve of my wife's painting, he added, or of her
marrying a man who wrote for his living: but they
were fond of her, oh so fond, and anxious to *help*. And
they liked me, too, it appeared, would like to get to
know me better; they thought there was probably a lot
of good in me, *when* they got to know me. Similarly,
he said, he had seen many old friends of *my* parents,
and they were eager to get to know Frida better, were
sure they would perceive things in her that they had
not hitherto noticed, if only they saw more of her. And
they were quite sensible, and stated openly that they
did not expect even to understand—or like—her paintings. It was so much better to be frank, like that, and
not to pretend, wasn't it?

"I am afraid he saw this line was not proving a suc-
cess, so he imitated Hitler again, in order to give himself time to think. We all three laughed a lot. Then he
told us about the last few bits of silver he had bought
before the war, and where he had sent them for safety.

Open the Door!

From that subject, he passed on to his life in the country, to his evacuees, and how it had turned out—you'd never guess, he said!—that my old tutor and Frida's governess were among them. They were always talking of us, telling stories of our childhood, and what *absurd* children we had been. 'Mind you,' he said, 'they're fond of you; don't think they're not.' Now he veered toward more congenial subjects.

"He confided to us what he ate, and what he drank. Sometimes, owing to the organizing genius of his cook, he had meat three times a week, sometimes four. Good meat, too. The cooking was good *bourgeois* cooking, and there was nothing better! On the whole, perhaps, he ate less than in peace-time, but he felt none the worse for it—if anything, better. (He had got into his stride by now, and at times stopped the flow, copious but deliberate, to regard us, most severely, to make sure we were paying attention. The slightest failure in this respect, the flicker of a single eyelash in another direction, he seemed in almost psychic fashion immediately to divine.) Often he drank cider now, he avowed, or ginger-beer, even. After all, it was war-time. And coffee, lots of coffee. He was called at 7.30, or, it might be, one or two days a week, at 8. . . . We seemed almost to be watching the hours going round.

"We did not speak: there was no necessity, he did not expect it. We did not dare, even, to catch one an-

other's eye. We gave—had to give—our whole attention, concentrate on the vast vista he was unfolding.
. . . Suddenly he broke off, looked at his watch, and
said:

" '*What* a time you've kept me here! . . . Why it's
ten, long past ten, and I see the waiters are trying to
clear away. We mustn't delay them. I always say it's
unfair on them to sit on and on. So I shall leave you
now. I ought to have gone an hour ago, for I'd promised, Robert, to go in and see your Aunt Muriel for a
few minutes on my way home. We often talk of you,
she seems so lonely and loves to talk of past days. . . .
Now you've made me be late.'

"He went to get his coat and hat and then, just as
we thought him gone, returned, to say, 'I forgot to tell
you, Frida, how I stuck up for you the other day. . . .
No, I won't tell you who they were, or what they said,
but I always stick up for you with everyone. You can
depend on that.'

"*He* had forgotten all about Natasha Danbury, I
think, and went home quite happy."

Robert stopped speaking, and we got up to go into
the theatre, for the next ballet, *Petrouchka,* had already
begun, and the puppets were moving their feet and
arms within the open booths, while the old magician
watched them.

Dead Heat

Looking back, the story of the friendship between the old Duchess of Martenburg and Princess Mouratinzky, the actual length of it, and the opposing points of view upon which it thrived, seems to me to possess all the fascination of a nursery rhyme, such as "Jack Sprat," or of a fairy-tale similar to the "Three Bears," exhaling in its essence a numerical, repetitive beauty implicit and continuous throughout its unfolding. . . . And for this reason I want to tell it to you.

I knew them both for what to me was a very long time, but, no doubt to them, out of their great age, merely represented the time occupied by the flashing of an angel's wings. . . . When I was a child, I first knew the Duchess of Martenburg. By birth a Princess of Southern Germany she had, with her wrinkled skin and brown eyes, rather bulbous now, albeit full of fire, all the charm of a well-educated and cultured toad, but a toad that was talkative, warm-blooded and loved dancing. (Indeed, she danced well, when I first remember her, though even then she was well over sixty.) With all the good-humour and high spirits of the Southern Germany of former uncontaminated days, she was witty in a straightforward way, and courageous: very down-right and sure of her own mind: further, she was religious, intensely devoted to her Church—rather unexpectedly, the Protestant Church of the North. According to the ritual of the seasons she moved with considerable pomp from one place to another, from one set of Italian rooms decked out with plaster cupids, red brocade, and pillared cabinets showing false perspective of tortoiseshell, coral and lapis, from one grouping of plumed fountains and cut trees, to another. . . . And every autumn, for a fortnight—the equivalent perhaps of a Catholic retreat—she came to England to stay with a bearded bishop, with whom, to the pride and pleasure of his wife and eleven moustached daughters, she was carrying on one of those mild flirtations so often manifested among the devout. . . . How well I remember her then, the parma-violet coloured velvet toque and dress which she always at that time affected, and the way she had of wrinkling her already wrinkled nose when she laughed.

But the Great War—still more perhaps the coming of Nazidom—had obliged her to alter completely her manner of life. . . . So that when I saw her again, after a lapse of twenty years, she had become a dignified refugee, banished from Germany because of her too great love for her Church, and because of her alleged consequent anti-Nazi activities. In the interval she had grown (and one could have expected nothing else) immensely old and very poor; for her, very poor. Nevertheless, she could still indulge in a certain style of living, for she dwelt now in a small *pension* on the very shore of the Lake of Geneva, and against this economical background, could still afford a maid (who, in any case, after fifty years would have refused to leave her), a footman and a sitting-room. But though her exile was easy, she resented her place of refuge. After the pleasant Bavarian Alps, these mountains seemed to her exaggerated and melodramatic. Despite her Lutheran affinities, she missed the graces of old Catholic Germany, the Madonnas on the corners of buildings high above the junctions of streets, the bunches of flowers upon the ledges of rustic shrines, the deep purple petunias hanging from the window-box of every window; things for which not all the blue and yellow tinsel stars of the Swiss spring sweeping over meadows and dark, damp earth, spread with scented pine-needles, could compensate her. . . . She was old, far too old for exile, she would say (indeed, she was over ninety), and what harm could a poor old woman like her have accomplished, she asked, even if she had been wicked enough to wish to injure her own country?

Still, one must make the best of it. The fish was good (those nice, pink trout); that was one thing. . . . And there were—yes, there were—a few nice people here. She admitted it; that was why she was at home every evening from four until seven. For at that early hour she retired for the night, being called at six the next day, and breakfasting on fine mornings at seven under a glossy-leaved magnolia by the side of the Lake.

Indeed, she possessed a fanatical love of fresh air, lived in it the whole spring, summer and autumn. Even in the winter in this climate, her windows were always wide open. Sometimes I used to try to soften her feelings concerning her place of exile, by saying to her how good the air was. "Look at the way you can sit out here under the magnolia all day long!" I used to urge, but nothing would mollify her. "I know," she would reply; "that is why I chose it—that, and to be near my dear old friend Princess Mouratinzky (I fear she is getting *very* old and infirm now, though she makes out that she is a few years younger than I am). But I do not like it: no, I do not."

Dead Heat

A different hurricane had blown hither the Princess. In her youth a great and famous beauty, even at her present vast age (for she was a contemporary of the Duchess, though, as we shall see, the vanity of former years prohibited her from boasting of this) she retained the manner and bearing of one; even a certain worldly wit, which sometimes goes with this kind of appearance and renown. Coquettish, alluring, full of *brio,* she talked continually, laughing and fanning herself the while—she was always opening and shutting a fan. And into the quality of her attraction still entered a great deal of feminine hard work, none the less arduous because it was unconscious. Apart from her animation, apart from her beauty, she might have seemed at first sight a more usual character than the Duchess; just a very pretty old lady with round blue eyes, beautiful and undimmed. But such a conclusion would have been false. . . . So far as her history was concerned, this fascinating old woman had become an orphan at an early age. Brought up at the Smolny Institute, she had, through the influence of the Tzarina of the day, been married on her seventeenth birthday to a great Russian nobleman and landowner, and had become one of the leaders of fashionable life in St. Petersburg. Subsequently, for thirty years she had been lady-in-waiting to the Grand Duchess Vladimir Constantine, and had been driving with her mistress in the second carriage, at the moment when that clever, gigantic monster, the Grand Duke, with his courage, his immense stature, his brutality and fatalistic wit, had been blown up by Nihilists as he was driving from a review of the Imperial troops. For a further twenty-five years until the Revolution, it had been her lot to comfort the beautiful and saintly Grand Duchess in her widowhood.

But the assassination of Russian royalties had now ceased to be an individual martyrdom, and had become degraded to mass-murder, a holocaust: (a dead man may leave his ghost behind him as a memory, but a dead army leaves none). The Grand Duchess herself, who had formerly been so beloved and respected, had now been murdered these many years, her body robbed and thrown into the Black Sea. . . . But fortunately her lady-in-waiting, the Princess, had been spending a holiday with a married daughter in the South of France at the time of the Revolution, and had so escaped sharing this fate, though the death of her mistress in such a manner was something from which she could never recover. It had been, in fact, more of a grief to her than the loss of her own fortune—for now she was penniless, living here, in the middle of a little Swiss town, in a boarding-house.

This establishment, however, was less unfriendly and impersonal than it sounds. Her daughter and son-in-law managed it, and they looked after her as well as they could. Her room, at the top of the house, was excessively small, and (though I think the Princess herself remained unaware of this) it had been in this same attic in which she was now dwelling, then cold and bare, that Lenin, a bitter fugitive, had existed for two years, working all day and all night, turning letters into cypher to send to Russia, writing endless pamphlets and books, eating nothing except when forced to do so by Kroupskaya, talking seldom—though when he talked a faint line of foam flickered from his sneering lips. Now, however, it was no longer a Swiss garret, for the Princess belonged so completely to her dead world of sleighs and furs and jewels and musical boxes, that everything round her still proclaimed her adherence to it. No sign of Lenin here now, only endless photographs, signed, of murdered Russian royalties; of the Tzar and Tzarina; the unfortunate young Tzarevitch and his three lovely sisters; Grand Dukes and Grand Duchesses and their children; photographs of the palaces and the gardens; photographs of them sleighing and skating and, for the rest, many brightly coloured ikons and bits of fur and lace—all that was left! But there was also a large stove, out of all proportion to the size of the room, and some small vases of flowers. . . . And these, for the momentary comfort they gave her (and all through that long life, after the manner of most Russians, she had lived from moment to moment), enabled her to bear her age and misfortunes more lightly.

For seventy years she had been the Duchess of Martenburg's most intimate friend. Neither of them had allowed so big a thing as being on different sides in the bitterest of all wars to make a difference to their friendship. There existed, nevertheless, *little* hindrances. Though they lived so near to each other—in order, they said, to be together—it was not easy for them to meet at all, and, further, it proved still more difficult for them, despite their mutual affection, to meet without quarrelling; because the Princess for her part rose at five every evening and retired to rest at five every morning. (You may ask how, in a neighbourhood not famed for the gaiety of its night life, she spent the small hours?) . . . Well, there was always tea and cigarettes; and often there were parties, for the boarding-house was full of Russian relatives and connexions, all engaged in trades which apparently obliged them to come in from time to time during the night—and, of course, to reach their work late. And so they clustered round the tall china stove, in the communal sitting-room, talking to the old lady; otherwise she would have died of ennui long ago. . . .

It was only, then, during that single hour between 6 and 7 P.M.—before dinner for the Duchess, and after breakfast for the Princess—that the two old ladies could meet. Nor was this the sole obstacle to their companionship even during that short space of time, all too brief, one would have said. For in the summer the Princess would not sit out in the garden with her friend; it was too draughty, very treacherous, she would protest. Still less would she remain out of doors in the yet hot but shortening evenings of the early autumn, when the mist rose from the Lake, like the wraiths of the murdered (certainly the Duchess's mind would never have entertained such fancies), and filled her bones with a chill depression. Sometimes at this season, the Duchess would insist on remaining out of doors, and so reaching a compromise, they would face each other angrily across the window-sill for nearly the full hour, handing cakes and tea sullenly across this bar which divided the Teuton from the Slav. In the winter, the Princess, fitted out in the remnants of a fur coat which, though tattered, still possessed a certain air, could only bear to sit in a room with the windows fast shut, and an enormous stove burning in it; while the Duchess dressed as though for a heat-wave, felt it essential for her health to have all the windows wide open. It was an especial offence to her, as well, that the Princess should live in an attic in the town, in the very heart of noise and heat and dust, when she might dwell in this glorious, cool air by the side of the Lake.

It was not easy, then, this friendship. To each of

them, their years had now become a source of pride. They had grown—though originally the contrast between their natures and outward appearance had been the foundation of the feeling between them—into rivals, competitors for the palm of old age, and, in consequence, the two old friends allowed themselves in this hour of frost for one, and fire for the other, to quarrel a good deal. . . . For, years ago, many long years ago, when the Princess had been forty, the, as it seemed now, needless fear of growing old combined with a certain vanity, had driven her to underestimate her age, so that even to-day, when she was in reality over ninety, her former deceit debarred her from any hope of ever catching up in the race. The Duchess, of course, knew her friend's age quite well, for it was the same as her own, but she intended to see that the Princess never staked a full claim, or that if she did, she would be convicted in no uncertain terms, and possibly before other people, of lying and self-pride. So she must remain a poor eighty-seven to the Duchess's self-avowed ninety-two; a sad eighty-eight to her ninety-three. Of course, even the eighty-eight to which she could admit was creditable, but ninety-three, ninety-three, ninety-three! . . . How deeply, how frequently, the Princess regretted that now so distant moment of coquetry! . . . Moreover, though she knew that the Duchess was well aware of her real age, she must never allude to it.

Dead Heat

On the other hand, the Duchess could, when it suited her, taunt her with it in a veiled way. . . . Sometimes when their conversation would be in English, a neutral tongue, for the Princess refused to talk German and the Duchess to talk French:

"Anastasie, I can't believe you are cold in that fur coat, and with such a fire! . . . But if you are so, why fan yourself continually? Even *I* should feel cold if I fanned myself the whole time! I'm sure that house of yours is unhealthy. . . . Perhaps you have a fever like one gets in one's youth."

"No, I can't help it, Rita, I always fan myself. It's like you, how you do all that embroidery, so pretty, with your good German taste! . . . Besides, if you suddenly feel hot, *you* can ask your maid to open the window for you; but I can't. . . . I have to do everything myself."

"But work is useful, Anastasie: fanning oneself is *not*. . . . Why, you fan yourself enough to turn a windmill: and at your age, it is not good! . . . But I forget, I was back in years long ago. You are younger, much younger than I am now, are you not? . . . You must look after your old friend. . . . How I wish you would come to live here in this glorious air, where you can hear the birds."

"But I do not wish to hear the birds, Rita. I ha-a-te them! They are so cruel, with their beaks! . . ."

Nor were these all the seeds of discord. The Duchess thoroughly disapproved of the Orthodox Church and all its ways, and though a service was only held in the minute Russian Church here, with its mad, painted domes and bulbs, once a month, and though, even then, the Princess did not attend it, since she was in bed and asleep in the mornings, the Duchess would often make pointed references to "mummery" and to "gingerbread places of worship," while the Princess would in turn feel herself called upon to defend the cause, and to attack in return the undecorative Lutheranism of Germany. Further, the Duchess would very seldom visit the Princess, would always insist on her coming to the *pension* to see her. This was because she pretended not to like Anastasie's daughter; it was a fiction, long kept up. . . . Really, I think, they had long grown fond of each other; but pride prevented them from publicly admitting by a reconciliation that their misfortunes had to this extent softened their natures. Nevertheless on the rare occasions of their meeting, they got on well, seemed pleased to see each other. When the Princess was unwell, however, the Duchess would continue always to say "That stupid girl of hers" (she was sixty-seven), "she does not look after her mother properly."

Then too, though originally the Duchess and the Princess had thought—or should one write, felt?—

alike, of late years the direction of politics in their countries had tended to separate them. . . . The Duchess possessed a radio, with which from time to time she fiddled, producing the sounds of whole covens of witches riding through the air on broomsticks over snow-covered peaks, shrieking, singing, screaming; she seemed, even, to like these sounds. But, occasionally, she would during that hour, and always by mistake for some concert or entertainment, tune in to one of the speeches of the dictators, and the Princess could, in those days (for it was before the Hitler-Stalin pact), no more help applauding the words of Hitler, who then saw "the Bolshevik demon" as the chief opponent of civilization, than the Duchess could prevent herself from showing enthusiasm at the utterances of the Paladin of Bolshevism when he so piously acclaimed democracy and denounced Hitler and persecution. Thus from six o'clock to seven would often grow poignant enough.

In spite of their differences of view, in spite of their disagreements, however, if either of them ailed or was unhappy, the other felt it as though it had happened to herself. Through the long days spent without her, though she was so near by, the Duchess would continually refer to Anastasie, her friend, just as during those long nights round the stove, drinking tea and smoking cigarettes through long paper holders, the

Princess would talk of Rita, her energetic and lively compeer. In addition to the warm feeling that existed between them, it became clear to those round them that the continued existence of one supported that of the other; they resembled the balanced scales of a machine finding an equilibrium, the equilibrium of truth. If one fell, the other would rise unduly.

Both, on the contrary, continued to prosper. The sensibilities of those who have lost profoundly become hardened except in small things, and the perpetual tragic developments of the 'thirties seemed now to worry them but little. They lost no faculties. The Duchess, in her charming way—in, even, her beautiful way—with her skin infinitely wrinkled and yet soft, her glowing brown eyes and uptilted nose, humorous and contemptuous and proud, grew still more ugly, her manners more typical, more imperative and abrupt: the Princess more vivacious, her blue eyes, still so large and full of light, more rounded, her white hair, that had formerly been golden, now still more white and soft—she seemed to smoke yet more cigarettes, as she sat in the corner by the stove, fanning herself, while through her head ran the nostalgic, circular melodies of Tchaikowsky, so that once more there came back to her the swinging movement of the Court Balls, the uniforms and crinolines and scents and swooping shoulders, the pink champagne, the whiskers, and dying hum of talk at the rattle and drumming of the tall golden maces on the floor as the Imperial Family entered the room. As though the exile which cut them off from the circumstances and places that had formed their characters had yet still further defined their respective traits, made each of them more typical, the Princess could now detect a draft at one hundred yards, the Duchess feel faint in the frostiest winter room if a jonquil scented it. The Princess would sit almost at the side of the stove, like a cat warming itself, while the Duchess would complain, even, of the heat of her unheated church. They altered little, very little: though the Princess would from time to time, shuddering in her furs, allow herself the indulgence of a cold, while eau-de-Cologne and smelling-salts would aid the Duchess's headache, caused—after one of her rare visits to the boarding-house—by Anastasie's stove. . . . For the rest the two old ladies were sound in wind, hair, eye and ear and tooth.

And so they lived on through the changing seasons by the side of the Lake, watching the glacial shadows of green deepen to summer blue, watching the magnolias extend white cups that later turned to tawny vellum on the glossy trees, the mauve chalices of the autumn crocus starring the lawns, until even the Princess could admit to ninety-two and the Duchess was undeniably within sight of her century. Both ladies grew more and more revered each year; for death is the chief—if last—dishonour to the living (and one which most of us will go a long distance out of our way to avoid), and so, in consequence, great age is everywhere honoured, because the overdue survival of any individual proves that in the long run humanity in the mass can lengthen, albeit only by ever so little, the normal span of its days.

Nevertheless the end was, naturally enough, drawing near. . . . This particular year had been, as usual, an unusual one. In March, it had been August; in May all the flowers of the vines had been destroyed by a hailstorm; in July there had been such a drought that the Lake had evaporated far enough down to show the lake-dwellings of paleolithic times, still fixed in primeval mud; September had exhibited the borders of the Lake again with all its luxuriant gardens flooded and drowned; and now, at Christmas (admittedly for once at the right season), came the Great Frost. The whole Lake was frozen over, a thing that had not occurred for a century, and people accepted the event with joy.

For a whole week the entire population skated day and night, with a strangely anti-Calvinistic fervour. Flares could be seen after dark, in every direction, gilding the flanks of the mountains, and bandsmen with faces and hands blue from cold, blared out Waldteufel waltzes, leaving a dragon's-tail of breath behind them on the air, while dumpy, Breughel-like figures, in their warm, padded clothes, danced and glided in ecstatic time to them. Huge fires were lighted on the ice, and oxen were roasted whole.

Frigid as was the air, the Princess could not resist this gaiety. And so, when it was at its height, she persuaded the Duchess to walk down with her to the edge of the Lake to watch the carnival. The Princess moved a little tremblingly with the aid of a very delicate, tortoiseshell-topped cane; the Duchess walked boldly, supporting herself with a stout country stick. The Princess wore her fur coat; the Duchess, a thick woollen outfit of some sort. It had not been long dusk; the fires were blazing, the torches flickering in a light breeze flecked with particles of ice. Both of them stood there in their snow-shoes in this icy world on the border of the Lake —on, as it were, the very edge of eternity—watching and listening. What a delightful scene!

"Do you remember the first time you came to stay with us in Petersburg, Rita, and all the bells ringing as we tore through the night on sleighs . . . and how we thought those times would never end?" . . .

"And that winter in Munich, the skating and the supper-party in the Pavilion?" . . .

She looked at her watch. "But that was all long ago —and now it is my bedtime." . . . Indeed it was ten minutes past seven, very late for the Duchess, and they returned to their homes, one plodding her way along, the other swaying a little on her feet.

It proved to be their last appearance together. The next day the Duchess developed a fever which she attributed to the heat of the fires, that had flamed, waving their golden wings, high above the ice; whilst the Princess was attacked by ague, due she said to the intense cold of the previous evening. Within forty-eight hours they were both dead.

Their illnesses were not painful, and merely seemed the ailments of two children. . . . It was nothing, the Duchess said, and would soon yield to fresh air. Through wide-open windows she had listened to the music on the ice and had enjoyed it. When darkness came, she would not have the curtains drawn, but watched the fires—which she considered responsible for her present state—being rekindled. At seven in the evening, the hour, originally, of her retirement, she sat up in bed and with great vigour asked her maid to push up the windows still further. To her surprise Elsa, the woman who had for so long attended the Duchess, did so, and then heard the old lady croak a few notes, harsh but gay: then the voice stopped, and, when she turned round, it was to find that her mistress was dead.

The Princess had not slept. All day long in her room, so high up, with glass misty from the heat, she had bent across the vases of anemones and narcissus to peer at the flying figures on the ice. From time to time she would retire to bed again, but always the distant sound of the music drew her back tremblingly to the window. The curtains were drawn as soon as it was dusk; the music only reached her faintly and she lay still. When she looked at her watch it was about six o'clock—she was late! It was past the time for her to begin getting up, she said. . . . But she was tired. She shivered, and fumbled with the things by her side, boxes, bottles, ikons. She pressed a button, and up out of a box sprang a little enamelled nightingale, moving from side to side with fluttering wings, and for a moment sang. She smiled and listened, and then, as it fell back into the darkness of its box, her heart, too, fell suddenly, and all her memories went with it. . . . Even from the neighbouring houses her relations could be heard crying the whole night long, and the whole of the next day.

Shadow Play

You must imagine three young girls, each an only child, all beautiful and all rich, immensely rich. They were not related, but among their parents prevailed that particular sentimental feeling, stronger than friendship, composed of intimacy, good-fellowship and complete interdependence, that exists only among the cosmopolitan-millionaire class. . . . Well, these three children had been brought up together, had played together, had spent each Christmas together, shared the same governesses, the same instructors in riding and dancing. Together they had learnt French, Italian and German (which, unlike the members of their mothers' generation, they could speak with fluency and correctness). They had been trained, too, to be "simple" and "unspoilt" and slightly infantile, as the super-rich like their children to be, but they had been taught nothing about how to manage their fortunes, how these had been amassed or why they should one day inherit them. Finally, they had been sent to the same fashionable finishing-off schools in Florence and Paris. Now they were eighteen, and the waiting earth lay at their feet.

With the hard, brilliant prettiness of a diamond, Zoe carried prettiness to an extreme. Her hands and feet were exquisite, and her voice, though in no way ugly, was so distinct it would have cut glass. Pauline was like crystal, a little larger in her loveliness, so clear but by no means soft, with the body and carriage of a young goddess walking over hills in the dawn, and a deep, throaty laugh. Her hands, too, were small and beautiful. Both of them looked out on the world: they fastened their bright gaze upon it with such eagerness that they saw nothing.

The third friend, Lorinda, was different. Slim and tall and dark and restless, her large mournful eyes looked inward on her self, and so sometimes she saw the world. Perhaps because of a latent softness of heart in that long, slender body, others, not of her sort, and living in the wild places beyond the gold bars, interested her: her blood beat in common with the blood of all human beings. In consequence, she seemed to herself among her own friends always a little unpopular, a little upon the edge of life. Being very young, moreover, though occasionally she made her own observations, she had not found out how to deduce from them.

Zoe, Pauline and Lorinda, in that dawn of the world as it was for them, spent much time together. It was as though this had been ordained. No one had ever suggested to them that they would be happier apart, and so they met continually, went on expeditions, visited shops and art-galleries together. Their mothers, as they played bridge of an afternoon in their drawing-rooms, so full of light, among the French furniture—signed pieces—and formal photographs of plumed and helmeted personages—signed pieces—and Ritz and Fabergé *bibelots,* said to each of them, in their tired voices, "All right, darling, you can go, so long as the other two girls are going. Don't stay out too late. And you'd better take your fur coat, and arrange not to be called too early. . . . And don't forget to come and say goodnight to Mummy before you leave the house."

That kind of life was only just starting. It was in the 'twenties, and the young and rich, if they would promise to remain content with the gold bars behind which they were fastened, would find their pleasures in plenty and brimming over. They would have, as their mothers said, "a glorious time." In the spring, of this, their first year, the families of Zoe, Pauline and Lorinda went to stay in Paris; they took up their quarters, two in their own houses, one in the Ritz. In May, they would return to London; after that, in the autumn, they would go to New York.

During this visit to Paris, then, there was to be one afternoon a sale of stuffs, silks and velvets and brocades, and the three girls decided to attend it. They had been there for about ten minutes, in an enormous, crowded, hot room, and Lorinda had been looking inside herself, not paying much attention to the frenetic yet dawdling tumult around her, when suddenly she saw Zoe and Pauline as though for the first time. Schooled in the arts of elegance though they were, they had for the moment shed these accomplishments. Their hands, always so cool and pretty, had become claws, like those of an Egyptian Hawk-Goddess, and all the possessiveness and greed of those ancestors, generation after generation, robber barons, Dutch from New York, railway kings and market-riggers, and New England farmers squeezing the last ear of wheat out of the soil, who had built up these vast fortunes now tottering under their own weight, manifested themselves in these furious, grabbing fingers, swollen by the excitement of possible bargains. Their eyes remained fresh and glittering as usual, their features, cameo-clear, but their hands grasped and wrenched and plucked and clutched and tugged at the stuffs on the counters.

And this appeared to be the point, too, at which the touching camaraderie of the super-rich broke down, for neither of the girls seemed, during this delirium of shopping, to be conscious of the other's presence— let alone of that of a third, and non-possessive, party. When they saw her, they elbowed her out of the way; she was nothing, thistledown. They, Pauline and Zoe, were worthy to fight between themselves for a prize, or bid in competition at an auction, where the race and reward is to the richest, but, for all her wealth, Lorinda, so their grappling, despoiling hands and knife-sharp elbows told her, must just keep herself out of the way!

Directly they left the shop, they were themselves again, with a well-defined sweetness and steely distinction, their hands pretty as flowers. But for Lorinda, the scene she had witnessed, retained an extraordinary, almost apocalyptic quality. These two other young creatures had become amazons, beings to be feared. Sometimes in nightmares she saw their hands turning the stuffs on the counters, pulling and grabbing them, feeling their web and the texture. The hands then held some fulfilment in them, a hint of menace that eluded her when she awoke, became vast raven-hued clouds overshadowing her whole future.

Open the Door!

Lorinda was young, and the lines of her life were as yet vague, unset. When she gazed within herself, the vista was indistinct; while outside herself, things seemed almost as she had been told they were; *almost,* for she was one of those who develop late, and already she noticed that they did not tally absolutely. How was it that she saw in some directions differently from her mother and her mother's friends? Why did the idea of staying in nearly every afternoon to play cards, so appal her? And what was the world for example, to which the work of the great musicians carried her; a world wherein her closest friends, Pauline and Zoe, appeared to have no part, nor her family, neither her father nor her mother?

But she only attained to the kingdom of art long after. . . . Now she was eighteen. Every night she attended dances, so as to meet the young men with one of whom it was supposed that after a few months, or even a year or two, in which to decide her preference, she must spend the rest of her life. A semblance of gaiety masked the seriousness which underlay these occasions. Huge awnings flowered in red and white outside the great yellow-stucco houses, and the rhythm of dance music, a beating and tattooing without tune, drifted out from them into the squares and gardens, and down to the hot pavements where always stood a few lonely watchers, silent, hungry, curious, their ragged poverty consuming with straining eyes these riches. On the balconies the young couples would look at them and say "What a funny old man down there!" and from top to bottom, rooms, staircases and halls were full of happy, meaningless chatter.

This kind of life seemed to continue for a long time, she could hardly tell, so confused did the delicious, long slumber of late hours render her, how long. . . . And gradually she found that she had fallen in love— or thought that she had fallen in love—with Ivor Harley, a young man who was shortly sailing for India with his regiment. It was understood between them that they should marry. He was young and gay and good-looking, and his eyes were full of truth.

He was leaving England in August, and so, some time soon, she must tell her mother, and then, next year, she would join him in Delhi, and they would be married. . . . She did not think that her mother would welcome the idea, for though he was rich, he did not belong to the super-rich; in whom, alone, virtue resided. It would be, she expected to be told, throwing her fortune away,—two fortunes, for one was to come to her from her father and one from her mother. She foresaw difficulties, but she knew she could obtain her parents' consent in the end, since it was a match to which no reasonable person of their world could object, and, in her own way, Lorinda could assert her dark, mute will, if her mind was made up. Besides, her mother, she knew, would like Ivor, for his good looks, his manners, his quickness. . . . She would tell them in August, before he left for India, but at present she did not want any awkward discussions to mar the happiness of their meetings.

However, in the early part of July a dreadful thing happened. Her mother died suddenly from heart-failure. The event convulsed Lorinda's whole life and outlook. To the young, death is so remote as not to exist at all and, in spite of the difference between their temperaments, she had always been very close to her mother. In the days that followed she had gone down to their country place with her father. She felt so sorry for him that she almost forgot about Ivor, though they exchanged letters; at first, every two or three days. As if the yawning of the grave had for the time chilled his emotions, the warmth in them had a little died down. She could understand that. No doubt he did not wish to intrude his own sentiments, did not quite know what to say, except to offer sympathy and continue to offer sympathy. She could hardly ask him here at present, so she would be compelled to go up to London to see Ivor, and arrange matters before he left. It would be quite easy, because the house was near London.

Under the grey and sulphurous skies that herald

thunder the early August heat brooded, lying heavy upon the gardens and the old trees, and in the large, hot dark rooms, padded with brocade and full of expensive objects, china, bronze, furniture, pictures, the loneliness of their lives became more apparent to Lorinda and her father.... The only thing that comforted her was the splendid way in which Zoe and Pauline behaved; kindness itself. She had written to Zoe, soon after leaving London, confiding in her about Ivor, and asking her to look after him, in case, without her presence there, his last few weeks in London should prove dull. And Zoe—it was evident from Ivor's letters —could not have taken more trouble to be helpful. While Pauline, in order to cheer her friend up, came to live with them for the summer and, with her practical nature, took off Lorinda's shoulders the domestic burdens of seeing the servants and ordering the food. (How much she hated these things! And her life would be full of them now, for, by her mother's will, she was already a rich woman.) In consequence, Lorinda was able more fully to give way to her grief. It was silly in a way, she knew, to grieve continually as she was doing. Everyone told her it would do no good and could not bring her mother back to life; but she could not help it. (Pauline was sensible and left her a great deal to herself: she appreciated that.) Her days were poisoned by the shock and by the sense of her loss, although they possessed a trance-like quality, unreal in the extreme. And she could not sleep. Uneasy slumber came to her for a few hours, but even then, full of dreams, sinister dreams, with grasping, dominating hands. . . . But perhaps they would stop when she went up to London to see Ivor. Her father, now that Pauline was here, could surely spare her for two or three nights! And she could stay with Zoe. She could not at present face her own home, after what had happened there. It really was kind of Zoe to stay on in London, right into August, when all the gaieties were over, in order to look after poor Ivor. . . . Lorinda thought of Ivor, and it calmed her. In her mind, she looked into the candid depths of those blue eyes, in which all truth and frankness dwelt, and presently she fell asleep.

The next morning she wrote to Zoe, explaining that she was obliged to come up to London for a few days the following week to see Ivor, and asking if she might stay with her? The reply came by telegram, "Certainly and may I motor to lunch darling with you tomorrow Zoe." Lorinda was enchanted. She longed to see her old friend again, and they could talk of Ivor. (He hadn't written, she remembered, for some days.) . . . It was curious, though, Pauline did not seem to be at all pleased when she heard that Zoe was coming down, and said something about how reluctant herself would have been to push her way in like that! . . . Rather silly of her, Lorinda thought, as she was there already. But that was only Pauline; she got into these moods sometimes. They meant nothing, so Lorinda let it pass.

When Zoe arrived, driving her own motor and looking enchantingly pretty and competent, they kissed, and then Lorinda took her into the garden. . . . The leaves lay heavy as cardboard on the air in the curious hush of full summer, no sound to be heard except the droning and hum of bees, which seemed, from the surrounding silence, to obtain a new and menacing tone. The enormous trees towered up, leaf upon leaf above them, toward the sullen, dove-coloured sky. It was very beautiful; a sort of peace descended on her at last, and as she walked between the huge green masts of the avenue, she felt a presentiment that all her life she would remember walking here with Zoe. . . . At first they did not talk much. How silent it was. Lorinda, looking at the leaves of the horse-chestnuts which composed the avenue, noticed how they extended toward her, motionless; (like swollen, stretching hands, she thought to herself). They made their way to a pillared temple by Kent at the end of the avenue, so that they could sit and talk undisturbed.

How lovely Zoe looked today, prettier than she had ever seen her, Lorinda decided. Zoe took off her gloves and placed them beside her on the old carved and painted garden seat. And Lorinda, who seemed to find herself nearer the surface, as it were, today, perhaps from the pleasure and surprise of her friend's visit, thought to herself, as she examined Zoe's hands, how silly—and jealous, too, she supposed—she had been before to imagine that, even for a moment, they had not been pretty. They were beautifully formed, slender, with almond-shaped nails. . . . Zoe was holding up her left hand at arm's length, staring at it in an absent-minded manner. What a lovely ring she was wearing! It must be new. Lorinda had never seen it before. It was not the *sort* of stone she liked, but it *was* a beautiful stone: her mother would have admired it, she thought with a pang; the pang of one who had forgotten for a moment the newly dead. . . . And so for a while she pursued her own sorrow, her own thoughts, not attending to what Zoe was saying. Zoe had put on her gloves again, and was laughing and talking almost too much. . . . Lorinda began to listen.

"So I shall sail for Bombay on the 7th of next month," she was saying.

"I had no idea you were going there," Lorinda interrupted, "but isn't it rather early? Won't it still be frightfully hot? . . . I wish you'd stay here. I shall miss you dreadfully, darling."

"But I've got to go. I can't help myself. . . . I was telling you! Ivor and I are to be married in October."

Pauline was horrified when Lorinda told her of it after Zoe had left. Lorinda had related it quietly, without comment. She was becoming trained to life.

"I should have thought her family would have stopped Zoe from making such a fool of herself," the other said; "after all, they're both very young. And he isn't such a rich man as all that. . . . I think you are well out of it, Lindy, if you ask me": Pauline continued, "but then young men bore me. *I* like people of experience," and she flourished a hand, a pretty hand.

At the time, Lorinda thought she was merely trying to be kind. But some time afterwards she saw her friend had meant what she said. For it was not until a full year after her mother's death that Pauline and her father announced their engagement.

*Idyll through the
Looking-Glass*

"*The service in this hotel* is shocking, very bad indeed," the Count pronounced. . . . And then, as though the remark were in some way connected with what he was doing or, further, had served to evoke his action, he rose from his chair to regard his image in the mirror opposite, first examining minutely eyes and mouth and nose, the innumerable connecting lines incised by laughter or anxiety, and then, sprucing himself, fingered his tie and touched the grey hair on his temples.

Startled at such an irrational outburst—as it appeared—of personal vanity, I, too, considered the features and the rather small figure reflected in the tall glass. . . . At any rate, he should be easy to recognize, I decided; except, of course, that he must have presented a very different aspect as a young man.

But then, somehow or other I had never thought of Count Dragone di Dragora as a young man. . . . Ever since I could remember him—and that was now for some thirty and more years!—he had looked the same, as though he had triumphantly defeated time by outliving it. . . . Not that he was old, any more than that —so it had seemed to us as children—he could ever have been young: he must have been born thus, found inside a cabbage, dressed in a frock-coat and high collar, and top-hat. And in my mind this diplomat, with, despite a rather tropical air, his Edwardian suavity and gloss, had been posed, always, against the contemporary London background of Grosvenor Square, hansom cabs—those equipages as frail and delicately balanced as the shell of Venus—and rooms full of palm trees and royal photographs in silver frames, so that it was with difficulty that I had accustomed myself to the idea that his proper setting had been one of prickly pears striking their attitudes from tufa rocks, of orange trees and lemon groves, and the smoke-tufted summit of a volcano. (Indeed, it must have been inside a cactus, rather than a cabbage, that he would have been found as a baby, according to the innocent deceptions of his period.)

Idyll through the Looking-Glass

All this had naturally lain beyond my vision, as a child of seven, but nevertheless, in his English surroundings he had been able to exercise upon my mind a very special fascination, an exotic charm such as would have attached to a Zulu chieftain or Red Indian brave; and, since Italians are invariably fond of children, we soon became most intimate friends. . . . How clearly I can see him, as he was then, when he came to stay with my parents in the country; moving among the croquet hoops in the summer, in white flannels with a thin black stripe, and a panama hat; in the winter, for shooting parties, dressed in the most elaborate check creations—English "sporting" clothes dramatized by a rich southern imagination, so that, on him, these garments were in no way ostentatious, matched his style, in the same manner that the mandoline-like twang of his accent in French and English—both of which languages he talked fluently and well—suited his speech. However, to one of my years, he had seemed vastly, immensely old, and, because we were such good friends, I have little doubt that I must often have told him so.

Of course, as I now rather covertly considered his reflection, I could see that he did look, after all, a little older; the lines were more numerous still than I remembered, and the frizzled hair, grown grey, made his skin of an even darker tint than formerly. . . . His whole appearance proved his descent as plainly as did his choice of clothes and personal adjuncts: for he was head of a famous Neapolitan family and possessed his share of Spanish and Sicilian, and so of Arab or *Saraceno,* blood. The whites of his eyes betrayed a curious dark, shadowy glitter, and his skin was very thick and yellow, like that of tough-hided, tropical fruit. Moreover, a southern love of jewellery showed itself in rings and tie-pins which would have pleased the Gabriele D'Annunzio of pre-war days. . . . Never before had I tried to picture him as a young man, and it had been a surprise to me to be told, a year or so previously, when the conversation had turned on the Dragon, as we affectionately called him, that, as a boy, he had been very good-looking, in the flowery, volcanic fashion of his neighbourhood. Nor had I realized, until I learnt it at the same time—for he always seemed, when I knew him, to have been destined for a bachelor existence, and the love-affairs in which he had been engaged (and to which, as I grew older, he made frequent allusion), had been those, plainly, of a very matter-of-fact, Edwardian order—that as a young man he had been of an intensely passionate and romantic nature, suffering deeply, continually threatening to emigrate, or to shoot or drown himself. It was as though, in his soul, the tender and amorous airs of the Italian seventeenth- and eighteenth-century composers had yielded to the rather sodden harmonies and tunes of Puccini, as though the scents of bath-salts and pomade had replaced the odours of jasmine and orange-blossoms in which he had spent his youth. Of his sufferings and passions, nothing was left but an immense tolerance for the weaknesses of others, and an intelligence which was intuitive rather than intellectual. But intelligent he certainly was, well-read in several languages, and with a fine taste in many directions: but all this he subordinated to life; his sole aim, perhaps, being to curb his sensitiveness, and so his powers of suffering, and only to make use of it sufficiently to enable him to obtain the most enjoyment out of existence.

Even after the Count had left the Embassy, he had always spent part of the year in London, as well as a month or two in Paris, Vienna and Rome. Friends welcomed him in every capital, for he was cosmopolitan in the mode of the day. European, more than purely Italian. And the reason for this, it may be, was principally that as a young man he had developed (if we may suppose a thing, so common to-day, to have, equally, existed then) an "inferiority complex"; because, if in those times, an Italian hailed from any part of the country south of Rome, he experienced certain disadvantages, even apart from the main one, that, in addition, he would certainly be poorer than someone

from the north of similar origin and situation. Moreover, Count Dragone could remember better times,
could just recall the old kingdom of the Two Sicilies
and its decaying court, the disintegrating splendours
of Caserta and of the capital itself: for he had been six
or seven years of age when the insurgent troops had
invaded Naples, and had finally driven the King and
Queen to Gaeta, where they had endured a long siege,
and then to exile; an exile which the Count's father,
as Chamberlain of the Court, had shared until his
death a year or so later.

A fate similar to that which overtook the rich families of the Southern States of America after the Civil
War had now fallen to the lot of many of the noble
houses of Naples, and specially of Sicily. Some became
destitute and disappeared entirely, while the palaces,
even of those who survived, lay empty. The long vistas
of rooms, with their pillared, marble-panelled walls
and mirrored ceilings, their periwigged busts of ancestors, the gardens, with their parterres and gesticulating
statues, stood deserted through the long, burning summer days, while the cactuses and circles of prickly pears
grew more thickly and violently round them, as though
to hide their present void of humanity with an African
pullulation of green life. . . . But the Dragone family
had been more fortunate than many of their friends

and relatives, and the Count seemed rich in a modest fashion, though—or, perhaps, because—he had never yet inhabited, since he came of age, any of his ten palaces that, now largely unfurnished, were scattered over the country from Naples to Syracuse, far across the Straits.

As a boy, he had lived with his mother, the old Contessa, in the smallest of his houses, situated at Sorrento; a little rococo pavilion, very elegant and old-fashioned, full of mirrors and tortoiseshell cabinets, with twisted tortoiseshell pillars crowned by little golden capitals, and of gilded chairs and Neapolitan pictures of the same epoch, displaying chiaroscuro processions of camels and turbaned drivers winding under palm trees, and many Madonnas melting into clouds. But, since I had known him, he had never until now visited any of his ancestral estates, had never ventured farther south than Rome, as though, indeed, he had feared that, were he to do so, the past would steal back upon him to his disadvantage. . . . When the war had come, however, he had returned to Italy, to make it his home. We heard that he had been working in some capacity for the Italian Government, and had settled in the capital, but otherwise we had, during that period, lost touch with him completely; as, indeed, with all our other Continental friends.

Open the Door!

It was not, then, until a year or two after the war that I saw our dear "Dragon" again, meeting him by chance one afternoon in this hotel in Sorrento. . . . I supposed he was about sixty: the mirror did not really, to my mind, register much change in him, apart from the details I have noted. He had seemed pleased to see me, if only, it may be, because of many visits, many years spent in England in younger and happier days, and overwhelmed me with questions concerning his friends. In return, he told me that he had been living here, in this hotel, for a whole year; during which time (for he was a sybarite by nature—as, indeed, he should be, since the site of Sybaris itself was in his possession and had for centuries belonged to his family) his own little palace was being prepared for him. Bathrooms and heating and electric light were being installed, carpets were being introduced upon the bare *terrazza* floors, and the furniture was being thinned out, and rearranged in a more modern mode. (Secretly, I thought these last improvements a mistake, but I was careful not to say so.) The workmen had taken six months longer than they had estimated already, and the alterations, apparently, were by no means as yet completed. . . . But he loved his house, he said, and would be quite happy there, would never want to go abroad again, even if he had been able to afford it . . . but think of the exchange!

Idyll through the Looking-Glass

"I never thought to return to Sorrento," the Count explained (how often have I wished that I could reproduce his voice, how much I long now to be able to treat his Italian accent phonetically, but these are tasks too complicated and beyond my powers), "but I am getting an old man. . . . Yes, I am, my dear boy, you know I am: I saw you examining me just now in the mirror. . . . Don't make excuses: it's quite natural when we haven't met for years—and in the end something drew me back. Do you know, it was over forty years since I had been here? I was nineteen when I left, and very different from what I now am. . . . Sorrento, too, how different it was! a joy to visit, for there was nothing like it in all Italy. You should have seen the lovely English carriages driving down the little Corso here, every bit as good as Naples itself, with smart English coachmen with capes and cockades in their top-hats, and horses and equipages all shining and varnished. . . . And even this hotel, in which we talk (though I seem to be doing most of it!), though smaller, was infinitely more agreeable, always full—and full of people the like of whom you do not see here now; people from England and France and Austria and Russia—and from America. . . . For those were the days when American girls were beginning to take Europe by storm, and they were lovely, lovely, with their beautiful, neat hands and wrists and feet, and their odd little voices and use of words. . . . There was something very strange about them to us Europeans: they showed such an unusual combination of boldness and prudery, of sophistication and naïveté. And such beautiful clothes; for they bought them in Paris, when English and Russian and Italian girls had to be content to buy them from the nearest town in their own countries. . . . (Ah, you young men laugh at such antiquated fashions, but then, you can have no idea of the *allure* of the dress of those times, the bustle, the small waist, no bigger than my neck, the fringe, the bonnet, trimmed with flowers or cherries, all full of style: and the rustle of the skirts as they walked.) . . . And such 'fun,' life was here (I love that English word, for which there is no translation): for many of us Neapolitans then still lived in our houses, and, you know, we are not the Tuscans or Venetians, who will seldom ask a friend, if he is a foreigner, inside their houses: but we, even when we are poor, give dinner-parties and dances and enjoy ourselves. So, though my mother, being a widow, entertained little, there was my cousin, Leo Casteleone, who received a lot, and Giuseppe di Bandanera and the Nestore di Noccras; then there were the Ouraveffskys, who had a villa here and were very generous and hospitable, like all their countrymen, and the Mellins, an American family, who lived up there on the hill, and then there were three English families, all cousins, the

Idyll through the Looking-Glass

Cleghornes, who were the great wine people and owned the whole valley and mountainside toward Positano; so there was always a great deal going on. . . . All this may bore you, but all the same, I must tell you, even the climate seemed better. It was never like today, with a cold wind—hotter, though not too hot (but we none of us ever felt the need of central heating, like we do now)—and the flowers, sweeter. In the evenings, from the terrace, which then only reached as far as that black rock down there—you could watch the little feather of a cloud, which always lay on the very summit of the volcano's cone, glow with an inner radiance shot with flame: (whereas now Vesuvius, like Europe itself, seems always either dead or in eruption). A thousand boats would gleam, in front here, on the softly rippling water, each with a bright lantern (such as our ancestors used to say the mermaids carried) to attract their prey, and every now and then the fishermen would beat the boards of the ship with their oars, for that sound, too, entices those poor, silly fish. The lights would seem a thousand glowing stars reflected in the water, the sea broke in the lightest foam upon the pebbles, as though in accompaniment to the serenade of the nightingales (how they sang then, day and night!), and over every wall was carried the heavy scent of orange-blossoms, on a sudden little warm breeze playing among the glossy leaves. . . . Whereas now, when you stand out there in the evening, all you can smell is petrol!

"And the hotel, though there were only two bathrooms in it (quite enough, people considered: think of it!), was so well managed. Never, as now, did a guest have to ask for anything twice. . . . Of course, I lived in our little *palazzo* with my mother, but I often came here to lunch and dine, though my mother—she was very old-fashioned and thought I should only know the people she knew—kept a strict watch on me; as strict a watch as she was able. I suppose 'our misfortunes,' as she always called them, the loss of her King and Queen, and the whole system of life—to which she had belonged—that had revolved round them, had made her proud: she was not what you would call a 'snob,' but she did not like the rich and the modern. According to her outlook, and to that of her ancestors, I must marry a girl whose parents she had always known, and whose grandparents had, equally, known mine throughout their lifetimes: that was the least upon which she must insist . . . and so, in the end, I never married at all.

"It was here that I fell in love (and though you never tell me your love-affairs, I tell you mine, for I am from the south); fell in love, you cannot imagine how deeply, how violently, with an American girl, Ethel Burkefield-Stoddard: to me, this was a beautiful name then, making my heart beat, my eyes flash. She was rich, an only child, and so beautiful: but we were never allowed to marry, for I was only nineteen, and my mother became very angry (she brought in those wretched priests to talk to me by the hour, and I, though my heart was breaking with love, had to listen to them with respect and attention): nor did Ethel's father like the idea, for I was too young, he said, and he would not let the millions he had made be wasted. I told him I did not want any money from him, but I think he disliked and distrusted all foreigners, especially if they possessed an old name. . . . But at any rate my darling loved me, though I say so myself, and though she was a little older than I was, would have married me, if only her parents had consented. Nor did she have any distrust of me—but then, she was not *like* an American girl, for she had a romantic and passionate nature, similar to my own in those days. . . . And, of course, I did not look then as I look now: by no means. . . . I would bring her every day enormous bouquets of flowers, and I believe her people laughed at me, saying they were taller than I was—for to present flowers was a Southern custom, not Anglo-Saxon: many hours, too, I spent under her window, for the whole world seemed full of music, and I could not sleep. Or sometimes I would hire bands of Neapolitan singers (and in those days, again, they were not merely hoarse beggars, trying to earn money by blackmailing our ears, but had lovely voices, soft and full) to serenade her. . . . And though to me, thinking over it all, thinking back, the whole thing is sad, it was at the time beautiful and wonderful and, besides, as I have said, 'fun.' . . . And then came a great quarrel between our parents, they took her away. . . . And though we had so often pledged our faith, our love, for all eternity, yet, as a matter of fact, I never heard from her, never heard of her, again. . . . Nor ever, after that, did I fall in love in the same way. . . .

"As you see, then, from what I have been telling you, I often came here. The entire place spells my youth to me. I know every inch of every path up the mountains, of every rock in the bay, where I so often used to swim. . . . But now, I never bathe: the water is too chilly . . . or perhaps it is my blood . . . I do not know. In youth, blood is hot, and one is strong": and the Count, after this typically Italian generalization, threw out and squared his shoulders, as if about to box.

"No, everything is different," he continued. "In those days, you asked for something, and it was brought before you had time to say—who is it, I forget, Jack Robinson?: but now, as I started to tell you, the service is very bad. You are left to ring the bell for ever; no one answers it. I have talked to you, *car' amico,* already far too long: but let me tell you, at least, about that.

"When I returned to Sorrento a year ago, I came straight to this hotel, and, though it seemed different and is, of course, double the size, at first there did not seem to have been such a big change—except that to-day everyone is so independent. . . . But it was just the same weather as it had been when I left, over forty years before, and at times I had almost the illusion that I had never gone away. (Such weather now is rare, but I did not know this.) As I walked in the town, many of the shopkeepers, and of the peasants, standing in groups by the market, recognized me and saluted me, and my tenants hurried to kiss my hand, so that I became proud, and thought, after all, it seems a very little time ago, and it may be I have not changed so much. . . . The hotel was rather empty: and, though the waiters seemed more numerous than the guests, none of them ever answered a bell: but they would rush about, in opposite directions, with napkins in their hands, looking very busy and occupied. . . . Well, one day I saw an old lady, very fat and lame, get up with difficulty from her chair, and waddle over to the mantelpiece to ring the bell. . . . No one answered. . . . So then I rang the bell for her, a second time. It was, as I have said, a very hot day, and she wanted a glass of iced water. But even when she had ordered it, no one brought it. So at last I became very angry, and I rang the bell again, and said: 'Unless that glass of water is brought immediately, I shall leave the hotel. It is a scandal!' And then, since they knew me, they were frightened, and brought it at once. . . . Well, that started an acquaintance with this poor old lady, for whom I felt so sorry, because she was so lame and looked so ill: and I think she was grateful to me, and liked me. . . . And I wondered, once or twice, how she had appeared when she was young, for if you stripped the fat from her face, and imagined a different colouring, she might have been handsome in her way. I asked her name of the concierge (she was a Mrs. Clacton-Biddle). Every day at luncheon, she would bow and smile, and perhaps, afterwards, we would exchange a few words in the hall, about the weather, or politics. . . . . Then, one day, I said to her: 'So this is your first visit to our beautiful Sorrento?'

" 'No,' she answered, 'I stayed here once before, long ago. . . . I should hardly like to tell you how long. Twenty-five years; a quarter of a century. . . . Just such days as these.'

"This interested me, and I said: 'Did you know any of the people in the villas here?'

"And she replied: 'Yes, I knew many of them: but they are all gone now, Nestore di Nocera, and the Cleghornes and the Mellins.'

" 'They were all friends of mine too,' I said, 'though, you must excuse me for saying so, but it is a longer time than you think, for it is over forty years since Nestore was drowned in this very bay. . . . I wonder if we ever met, for I lived here too then?'

"But she was thinking to herself, and paid no heed to my remarks. There was a smile of reminiscence on her face, which lit it and made it momentarily assume a certain familiar beauty, and yet one which I could not identify in my own mind: though now I saw that she must, indeed, have been beautiful in days gone by.

" 'They were all friends of mine,' I repeated.

" 'And then,' she continued, 'there were the Ouraveff-skys and the Bandaneras; so many friends: and my particular friend, Count Dragone di Dragora: but he is dead, too, they tell me.'

" 'Madame,' I cried, 'everything you tell me is true except that. Count Dragone di Dragora is not dead: he stands before you!' . . . And then I saw who she was, this fat, lame old lady. . . . It was Ethel Burkefield-Stoddard: and, as her eyes rested on mine, just for that one instant I heard all the nightingales singing again in the glossy darkness of the orange trees. . . ."

"But do you know the queerest part of it: afterwards, now that she knew who I was, it seemed as though she wanted to put a barrier between us? . . . She became more distant in her manner, grew unwelcoming, and

spoke to me little. . . . I do not know why. . . . Perhaps
—who knows?—she regretted our intimacy; perhaps—
indeed, surely—I disappointed her, and she bore me a
grudge for it; perhaps she felt a different person herself, and thought I knew too much about her; or,
again, she may have wished that, as she now was, I had
never recognized her, and thus been forced inevitably
to match against her present appearance the image of
her which I must remember from past years. . . . Or
perhaps it was merely that she had been married—and
widowed—in the interval. . . . I do not know. . . .
But, after a time—shorter, I believe, than she had intended—she left, and sailed home from Naples. . . .
And, since then, I have received only two letters from
her; the first to ask me to obtain for her one of those
red lacquer boxes—you know the kind—that they
make here—in which to keep her handkerchiefs: and
the other, remote and bleak and impersonal, to thank
me for having sent it. . . . It was all such a long time
ago, I suppose."

The Count stopped talking, and looked in the glass
again. And for a moment I, too, caught a glimpse of a
person lost long ago; a different dragon, warm and
with a soft shell. And then again, it hardened into
everyday armour.

Champagne for the Old Lady

One of the most peculiar qualities of gambling is the power it possesses to make even the laziest man work hard, if only for a limited period; the period being, of course, limited by the money he has—or can borrow—to lose. Any gambler will toil through long, exhausting hours until daylight creeps cruelly through the curtains to reveal columns and shafts of cigarette-smoke and a suffocating atmosphere in which only germs could thrive; toil, at that, only in order to squander as much money as he could gain elsewhere by honest work in an infinitely shorter time. . . . Certainly I laboured far harder in the Casino—or "the Studio," as, for that reason, I preferred to call it—than I do now in writing this story.

239

Open the Door!

Roulette was the game. We were both of us far too poor to afford to gamble, and we both liked to lose our money in different ways. John Treguze had invented a real system for it, and whenever he had lost at the tables the whole of the money he had taken in with him, he would comfort himself with the same vague sentiment: "It's no good breaking off now. I ought to give my system a fair trial." As for myself, I relied for my efforts upon intuition—a gift which can prove quite as expensive as any more intellectual method, for he who is endowed with it just scatters the counters over all the numbers that catch his eye or take his fancy. On the other hand, should he win, the laurels that crown prophecy are added to those of triumph.

We often argued the faults of our various ways of play. To begin with, I would point out to John, his methods were too complicated: for, if you were determined to experiment with a system, this necessitated taking with you to the table an immense quantity of counters of every sort, from ten thousand and five thousand francs down to hundreds and tens—far more than you could afford to lose; but the possibilities of a system, a thing so high above mere chance, justified in your mind the slight risk, as you saw it, of losing them. Indeed, it became a duty. (If you had lost heavily before, it was not because your system had betrayed you, but because you had not played it long enough.) And then, always just as the end to which you had so long been progressing was at last beginning to come in sight, human frailty entered too; either you forgot for a single throw to back one of the essential numbers, or the ball might be started over-soon, so that you were not given the time in which to complete your usual lay-out of counters, or you found that you had already, without noticing it, lost all the money you had brought in, and so were obliged to miss the very spin that would have made your fortune. Whereas my lack of system—which, in itself, almost amounted to one—was simplicity itself, easy to manage: you took as many counters as you wanted, placed them where you liked, and when you had forfeited them all, you either left the building or obtained some more—and lost them in addition. No fuss or brain-fag. . . . Nevertheless, at times when I scanned John's face, looked at his dark, luxuriant hair, his regular and determined features, his eyes, that, though short-sighted, were so far-seeing, or regarded his large frame, his system seemed to me so well to match and express his physique that I wondered whether he might not win with it after all.

That night at dinner, on the terrace in front of the hotel, we discussed these problems again. Dinner lightened the sense of our losses: it was a warm night of early summer, and the grass, of so vivid a green, and growing singly from the soil like the tenderly nurtured hairs on the head of a bald man, the flowers and palm trees and kiosks and cupolas of this holy city of chance, presented the enchanting vistas of a mid-Victorian stage-setting. And all this beauty had been created out of the money lost by gamblers! We began to feel that we, too, had "done our bit" toward it, for this evening we had been victims. . . . But soon, over our brandy, we began to talk of other things, until it was nearly time to go, to start again. . . . John chose a cigar—to smoke later, he said, when he was winning, for it helped him to keep his head cool: and then we spoke of cigars, how expensive in France and England, how cheap and good they were in Holland and Germany—and in Austria; where, he informed me—for he had at one time lived there—even women, and especially those of the former, aristocratic régime, smoked them in preference to cigarettes. . . . I wondered if I had ever seen a woman smoke a cigar in England? . . . But I was sure I had not, for it would look so odd that one would remember it.

We walked across to the Casino and found its marbled saloons, smelling so strongly of post-offices and old scent, unusually crowded, airless to the point of suffocation. A pleasure cruise had touched here this afternoon, and the pleasure crusaders were standing round the tables in staring groups, ox-eyed with Swiss or Scandinavian wonder, and getting very much in the way of the habitual, as it were resident, gamblers: those old ladies with delicate complexions enamelled over thousands of cobweb-like wrinkles, with many veils and bags, and a slight, harassing twitch, who, harmless old flotsam of Edwardian days, compose the steady population of such places. Little processions of black-clothed croupiers, with down-turned eyes, like the mutes at a funeral, marched through the rooms, guarding a coffinful of counters.

The public rooms were too thronged to-night for John to be able to obtain the share of the croupier's attention which his system demanded: besides, it was far too hot and one felt penned-in at the table, as though a sheep-dog would soon round one up, so we entered the Salle Privée, usually to a certain degree free of tourists. It was now about a quarter to eleven, and the gambling was in full swing: it seemed much cooler, though we found that the cruising parties had even penetrated here in their urge to gape. In addition, there was, of course, the usual Salle Privée circle of old witches, with tousled white hair, sitting round the table, staring at the wheel, mumbling spells and curses through nut-cracker jaws. They never played themselves now, all their losses were in the past, but they paid still to enter in order to inconvenience the real players as much as they could by taking all the chairs, so that the others had to stand up, thus too far from the table to be able properly to place their stakes. John, however, found a good seat, next the croupier, and began sorting out and arranging his columns of counters as a preliminary. I stood for a moment to watch. The old lady who had at the same time taken the empty chair next him, attracted—and held—my attention. She differed so greatly from those all round her who so plainly lived in the town and made this their headquarters. Unused as she must obviously be to the Casino, she looked too good—too *morally* good, I mean—for her environment. Well over seventy, I should say, she was slight in figure, her complexion was that of a girl of seventeen, and her eyes still had a youthful, meaningless caress in them when she looked at you. She was dressed quietly in black velvet. A sort of black lace mantilla framed her head and flowed over her soft, white hair, being tied in a wimple under the chin, thus emphasizing a profile that was, even now, of a du Maurier-like calm and purity; and she carried, as her only impedimenta, two fans, one painted, the other of black lace: these she put down on the table by her. Regarding her, one saw that she was, in fact, one of those rare creatures, an old lady who, besides retaining her beauty, had retained her prettiness; a far more difficult achievement.

I reflected how lucky John was to find her as a neighbour instead of one of the usual, clawing harpies of the Casino, and then left him, in order to have a drink in the bar. There people were swallowing coffee and cock-tails and brandy and every sort of drink for every hour. For a while I listened to their desultory fragments of talk. An elderly, voguish American gigolo with very smooth, black hair, and hands flapping like a seal's flippers, was seen remarking to a much older American woman, dressed in a low evening dress of white lace sprinkled with pink roses, "My dear, it's chic, and it's *soignée* (swànee), but it gets you nowhere!"

When I returned to the table John was immersed in his system and had lit his large cigar. Smoking was, of course, allowed, but I noticed (as he did not, for he was too busily occupied) that the pretty old lady next him, with her soft white hair and large, soft blue eyes, had begun to show symptoms of distress, to cough and fan herself gently. John's great frame, posed next to hers, served to make her look still smaller and more shrinking. The coven of Casino witches round the table, with their gnarled, veined, grabbing hands that might have been carved from the root of a box tree, their hard faces and circular parrot's eyes, seemed by no means impressed by this display of sensitiveness, and glared cynically at the victim (this, no doubt, would have been their attitude at any show of natural feeling), but the strangers near by, and the barricade behind her of Scandinavian and Swiss tourists, soon became interested and sympathetic, solicitous on her behalf. What a shame for a great big man to smoke a huge cigar like that, next to her, their faces said plainly! Probably in the old French *manoir* whence she must have sprung, she had never even seen a cigar, far less smelt one. (How curious, indeed, to see a lady of that kind in the Casino at all: she was not at all of the type they had expected to discover; must, somehow, have wandered in here by mistake.) But that was the rich all over, trampling on the feelings of the poor and re- fined. Why, though she was sitting down, if you looked, she was not even playing! Too poor to afford it, that must be the explanation. There was self-restraint for you! But you did not see people of that stamp nowa- days; too gentle and good for this gas-mask, weakest- against-the wall world.

The old lady was by this time fanning herself vigor- ously, first with one fan, then with the other. She would take one up, and then put it down again on the table, near John's counters. Her manipulation of these instruments was wonderfully expressive. Like that of a geisha, or a great Chinese actor, every movement bore its burden of significance. She turned her exquisite profile away from her neighbour, and his vile habits, as though to obtain air. By now the cigar and the system were well under way, and I do not think that, until this minute, John had been at all aware of the growing interest and disturbance round him. But suddenly the old lady became vocal, began to complain audibly, partly to herself, partly to the crowd, in beautiful old-world French: and the crowd started to take her side, to murmur in their various doric tongues. (As she spoke, I wondered was there not, after all, a hint of foreign intonation in that telling, vibrating voice; was not the use of idiom a little too perfect for someone speaking her own language?) The croupiers alone remained unmoved, their eyes glazed with fatigue and boredom, or with a slight, furtive and reminiscent smile hovering round their colourless lips, according to their types. Now she fanned herself almost truculently for one of so gracious a personality, grimaced, showed her distaste in many evident ways, and finally made an open protest to the croupiers and the world in general. The croupiers remained silent, indifferent, but the world in general responded. Once more she appealed to the nearest croupier, who, waking himself from a despondent trance, in which, obviously, he despaired of humanity and its greed, declared that he could do nothing; smoking was allowed.

She demanded to see the *chef-du-parti,* and plied the fans incessantly, taking them up, putting them down, holding them at angles, in order to protect herself, and using them to attract the crowd's attention and to point out to them the delinquent. Meanwhile, John had grown conscious of the tension in the air, and had become thoroughly annoyed, for his neighbour had created and worked up this scene without ever addressing a single request to him personally: so he continued to smoke, and endeavoured, against increasing odds, to maintain outward calm and to concentrate successfully on his complicated system of gambling. Eventually, however, the muttering and the general, carefully cultivated feeling of antipathy toward him affected his nerves, and, turning toward the pretty old lady, he offered to put out his cigar, adding that he would have been delighted to do so at any previous moment had she seen fit to ask him. She did not even reply. It was too late: she was offended beyond repair. Elegantly, with conspicuous grace of carriage and dignity, she collected her fans, rose from the table, and glided out of the room in a rustle of resentful black velvet. The onlookers glared furiously at John, who, in return, blew out defiantly a small cloud of smoke. Poor old lady, they said, to treat her like that. What a shame! A great big brute, with no respect for age or delicacy. But how truly she had shown her breeding! How beautifully she had walked out, without a word! Why, she could not have done it better if she had practised it for years! There was a real lady for you! You didn't see that sort nowadays.

John certainly felt uncomfortable at her ostentatiously quiet departure (moreover, he had been losing again for some time, though he had begun well this evening, when he first arrived. Because gambling has an element of exhibitionism in it; the player, to win, must compel the wonder and admiration and even envy of the spectators. Their disapproval and dislike will ruin his game). The whole affair had depressed him and spoilt his evening—but it was not until ten minutes or so after she had left that he realized that all his high counters had gone with her. The better system had won.

The pretty old lady, I was told afterward, was an Austrian, in spite of the elegant and lovely French she spoke. And it was her custom always to select an evening when the rooms were crowded with Swiss and Scandinavian naïfs for the testing of her system. The smoke-screen was a regular trick, and one that usually worked well, since large cigars and quantities of counters seemed to go together in the Casino, like the chatter of a conjuror at the moment of counterfeiting his magic, her protests were designed to distract the attention, both of her audience and of her chosen dupe, from the sleight-of-hand which was in progress before them. The opaque film from the cigar resembled, too, the cracking of the magician's pistol, while the smoke itself afforded some disguise, comparable to the cloud of ink thrown off by an octopus when engaged in combat, in order to mask its manœuvres—except that, in this instance, it was the octopus, still more wily, who compelled her prey to emit the concealing veil. But, had she been ejected by the authorities, doubtless aware of her game, a riot would most surely have ensued, so firmly did she always establish herself in the hearts of the onlookers.

I did not stay in the Casino long enough that evening to see the end of John's system. (We were leaving the next day.) The rooms were far too hot, and I strolled out toward my hotel. It was delicious. The feathery palm leaves lay motionless on the air, laden with the scent of orange-blossom and strong-smelling night flowers. On my way back I passed a large café, like an illuminated conservatory, with a uniformed Tsigane band stationed near the entrance, playing waltzes. The chairs set outside looked so inviting that I took one and ordered a drink. In the opposite corner sat the pretty old lady, nodding her head in time to the waltz the band was playing; she had evidently just finished her supper; an empty half-bottle of champagne stood in a silver pail of ice by her side. And, as I got up to go, I noticed that in the manner of many compatriots of her sex in the old days, she was just lighting a cigar.

Long Journey

In the Tuscan towns the sound of trams creaking, their bells ringing, and of open exhausts of motors blare down the narrow streets, at sundown; streets, tawny as a lion, but in which it is nevertheless impossible to observe the full drama of the autumn, so intense on the outskirts and in the country behind, where it drags a hem of purple over the dusty hills and into the woods of ilex, the leaves of which glisten like the glossy, night forests in the canvases of Uccello. Through the middle of each town flows desultorily a dwindled yellow river. The palaces, balanced and proportioned as a mathematical formula or a problem in Euclid, hang above streets, too narrow, again, for the passer-by to be able to judge of their pure, incredible beauty, now for the most part remote and dead as that of the Parthenon or of the clustered, broken towers of San Gemignano. The streets, for all their bustle, are similarly dead; it is the activity of the devouring worm more than of life itself. The palaces, except for the cobblers and fruit shops on the ground floor, are dead too; but the cobbler hammers all day long at his last, and the old women, who gossip or haggle over *soldi,* peering from behind their autumnal mounds of green figs and purple figs, of grapes and of orange persimmons, fit into these elegant, slightly rusticated arches so well that they seem as much part of them as a snail of its shell. . . . Up above on the *piano nobile,* either a dressmaker, as if engaged in black magic, stabs a silken bust with pins, her mouth still full of them, or a lawyer interviews his sullen peasant client, so unable to explain himself, or an American is giving a cocktail party. For the most part, the former owners, whose names have echoed down the centuries from the time of Dante— just as a footstep now echoes through the mirror-like view of door after door, ceiling after ceiling, room after room—have disappeared, have sunk, like stones to the bottom of these clear pools, leaving only the enlarging circles of their names to float upon the darkening surface.

The Palazzo Corineo, however, is an exception. Built

by Alberti, it lingers, with reproachful perfection, in a crowded by-street: where its fragile arcaded façade, one of the surviving wonders of the world, hangs almost out of sight, so that the lover of beauty who wishes to examine it will very soon be hooted out of his survey by a motor-car or belled out of it by a cycle. Herein, however, the descendants of those who caused it to be built still live far down their endless pillared vistas; there are footmen in livery, and a vague air of the Eighteenth Century still attends upon the public goings and comings of the old Prince and Princess. Yet even for them the view here is one that diminishes year by year, uncertain to the point of certainty; for they are childless and have few relatives. The last palace will soon be uninhabited.

The Prince, a quiet, bearded scholar of the mandarin type, sad and floating above the life of the day, possesses manners as formal and beautiful as the rooms in which he lives: but the Princess, on the contrary, opposes to them a different and ebullient system of life, a different upbringing, a different set of manners. A Russian Princess in her own right, a Cossack by blood and inclination, she was born during the Court Ball in the Winter Palace, and was, so she says, baptized in a golden ice-bucket filled with the pink champagne reserved for the use of the Imperial Family. This indomitable old lady remains unaware that she appears as much a stranger to the present day as would a Princess of Byzantium. The double-headed eagle still flutters its wings about her: her hoarse, interminable chuckle fills the dead rooms with life. Many of them she has reduced to the level of an Oriental bazaar; Russian silver and ikons, jewelled watches and boxes, tinsel brocades, swinging censers and the endless junk of that lost civilization litter and clutter-up the delicate, finely counterpointed perspectives. . . .

The Princess's day is a full one. Every morning she rolls for half an hour on the floor, to keep her back straight and preserve her suppleness. Then she has to dress, a complicated process, arrange her wigs and eyebrows and colour her complexion. Her morning is divided between prayers and the samovar. About twelve, the ravages of time repaired as far as she can repair them, she comes downstairs in all her full splendour. But by this time the Prince is working, disentangling the pedigrees of noblemen long perished, restoring order down these other perspectives of time; arches which have collapsed beneath their own weight and have become overgrown. (Italian culture resides in these finely balanced vistas which it has invented, vistas of rooms, vistas of music—each note echoing under a vault—vistas of the theatre, fading and illusionary.)

Luncheon is at twelve-thirty, and they eat often alone, one at each end of an immense table. All through the day, the table-cloth, very large and very white and clean, is left on the table and is thickly encrusted with glittering, bulbous Russian silver, with silver roses and silver flowers (the dowry of the Princess); even Nanina, her fringed and fussy dog, eats in its own corner off a silver plate.

For the Princess, the day begins with the afternoon, when she goes out driving with Nanina and Count Ranucci, her *cicisbeo* (for she is one of the last to preserve this Italian habit). Barricaded against the wind behind a cockaded and cloaked coachman and footman, wearing Russian caps of fur, they drive interminably through the public gardens, round and round that delta between the two yellow rivers, arguing, laughing, quarrelling at the top of their voices, while Nanina snarls and motors whizz and hoot past them. Then come interludes of tea-parties and cocktail-parties, or else the Princess receives until seven—when, unless there is a ball, which happens very rarely, the day ends for her and the night swallows her up. She dines alone with Nanina and the Prince, or with Count Ranucci. When the Count is there, the Prince goes to bed, where he dreams of climbing family trees and swinging from heraldic branches. With the Count, her loved Pepino, the Princess plays bezique in her boudoir until two or three in the morning.

Even in warm weather the room is very hot from a

porcelain stove, and the chuckles and laughter, and the angry interludes, are wheezy as the asthmatic breathing of Nanina in her tight-laced coat; that odious, corseted dog, with her false voice continually rapping out commands and saying things which she does not mean. And Nanina is always hiding, always having to be called, replying with a horrible yapping, the direction of which she yet contrives to disguise, so that both her mistress and her friend have perpetually to rise from their game and hunt all through the long, dark vistas. Ever, with one exception, since the Princess married and came to live here nearly sixty years ago, there has been a Nanina: and it has always looked like this, twelve years old, with a pointed, dancing-master nose and a corseted bust, an air of busy, fussy command, wheezy but inconsequent.

I could never make out to what breed Nanina and her four or five predecessors belonged, but it appertains obviously to the 'sixties of the last century; a breed imported into the cushioned, silken boudoirs of Russia from the palace of the French Second Empire as a sign of western culture and emancipation. When not carried, the feet of this dog seemed to rap out, like a step-dance, the mid-nineteenth-century French airs of Delibes or Offenbach upon the hard, polished *terrazza* floors of these unending vistas. . . . Sometimes I think that Nanina, the apparently eternal, is, despite her western origin and affinities,—in this comparable with the mounds of Russian silver and jewelled dolls—but another symptom of the emphatic opposition the Princess offers to the classical and orderly life under the arches and coffered ceilings of her palace: for the Princess's blood must ache at moments for the gipsy wailings and the songs from barges, for the immoderate and unmodulated landscape of Russia—so large as to have no perspectives—for the glitter and illusion of the Old Régime, for the bulbs and spires and crowns of the Kremlin and the amethyst-quartz grotto of the frozen gardens of Tsarsköe Selo.

One evening I sat with her, drinking honey-tasting tea and eating complicated sandwiches (for the Princess loved people to be with her, and especially the young—indeed, she was always kind to them and liked to examine them about their love-affairs). But for my presence, indeed, she would have been alone this evening, for there were no parties in the town, and she had indulged earlier in the afternoon in one of her violent, recurrent quarrels with Pepino, that large, big-featured *punchinello*. Through the door of her little sitting-room, crowded with ill-assorted objects (a room which, in its essence—though not, perhaps, in its profusion—so much resembled the dressing-room of a great theatrical star), I could perceive the darkening vista of the grand *salas,* room after room, *sala* after *sala,* empty, sad and echoing, yet full of beauty and courage and vision. Usually their extraordinary quality vanquished the human interest of the people who had lived in them: you did not wonder concerning them, did not muse about the succeeding generations, in armour, in striped hose and doublets, in wigs and velvet, in crinolines and panniers, who through a lifetime had walked down these perspectives until finally they reached the past, or try to catch the dying sound of their voices, their accents echoing down through their descendants in the same way that, in their own day, they had echoed up into nothingness under these high ceilings.

It was a warm evening as we drank our tea. Our room alone blazed with light, and from those beyond were wafted darkness and cold and, somehow, a feeling of expectancy. . . . Someone out there, one might have thought, was waiting for us—or were we waiting for someone? There was a crackling outside, and Nanina creaked her bones about her and barked. . . . A ghost, I wondered: and I recalled that the palace was haunted? . . . I forgot the story, though so few Italian palaces are haunted that you would have thought this tale would have been easy to remember. As I talked, I tried to recollect what it was, and to what age the haunter belonged? . . . Not later than the time of Napoleon; because this whole system of life had died with him and Stendhal. Now the owners possessed no souls to leave behind them, were only animated shells, for all the Princess's energy. . . . Certainly upon this evening the past seemed nearer than the present. . . . After a time I gave it up, and asked the Princess openly about the ghost, and if she had ever seen it? . . .

It had belonged, apparently, to the age of Romeo and Juliet, a fifteenth-century apparition, a girl who had died for love of a man whom circumstances forbade her ever to see, for he was a Guelph and she was a Ghibelline, or *vice versa* (indeed, I *ought* to have remembered, for she had been famous for her beauty, and her name was a household word here). It had been a romantic love, of swords and flowers and cloaks and serenades; a fifteen-year-old girl, with golden hair braided round her forehead, and with the dark, golden skin, slanting blue eyes and softly moulded aquiline nose of the Tuscans. There had been a portrait of her in the palace, but it had been sold and carried off to America more than thirty years ago. . . . Only the house itself remained, and its shadows, living and dead.

Even as we talked, it seemed to me, at any rate for the moment, that the air began to inspissate and thicken, to become colder; every teaspoon taken up or put down redoubled its tinkle; every plate was moved with a thud. The house seemed, more than ever, to be waiting. It was the hour of silence before the innumerable sounds of the Italian evening begin.

Open the Door!

"No, I have never seen the ghost, the poor thing," said the Princess, "but once, long ago, I heard her voice. It must have been soon after I married, and long before we sold the Botticelli portrait of her to instal the electric light. (Now, you see how comfortable it is!) It was an evening like this, and in those days, after Petersburg, it seemed quiet here, and I was restless. I remember what a beautiful disturbing day it had been, like this one; I could not sit still as I do now; I suppose it was my nomad, Tartar blood. The Prince had gone out, and my dog, my first dog, who was called Tita (though my husband didn't like my calling her that, because it had been the name of his ancestress, the ghost, the famous Tita), had disappeared, just as Nanina does—Nanina, darling, where are you?—and I could not find her anywhere. (She is always so naughty, my beautiful angel! Although my Tita has long been dead, she was just the same to look at, though not so lovely—no darling, not so lovely!) The sun had not long hidden itself behind Santa Croce opposite, but it became very dark in this house and I walked through room after room, calling 'Tita! Tita! Tita!'; but there was no sound of my dog, not a bark from that angelic, furry throat. My voice echoed strangely under those high ceilings that were now so black, and little breaths of cold air swept over the bare floors. Even my footsteps echoed, and if I had not already come to know the rooms so well, and how they were disposed in a square round the court, I would have been afraid of losing my way. . . . Still I went on calling, calling, until the whole air seemed full of the cries: 'Tita! Tita! Tita!' . . . You know, I am a Cossack, and I am not nervous. At the age of seven I saw the peasants riot and try to burn our house, and did not flinch when they were beaten and mown down. I have —how do you say it?— no *fancies*. . . . And yet the number and size of the rooms, room after room, their coldness and darkness, began to weary me. In the furthest *sala* one window was open, and the blue dusk came in at it. I wondered for a moment, as I entered, if I saw a figure standing by the balcony? . . . There was nothing. . . . I called again, 'Tita! Tita! Tita!' . . . And, suddenly, a voice, a lovely, golden, warm, Italian voice, sounding, though, as if, in spite of being in the room, it came from a great distance, down a vista of centuries, answered me: 'Here I am, here I am! *Eccomi!*' and then seemed to diminish—diminuendo—and die away back into those endless years down which it had travelled. After that, the silence gathered round again, and no sound except the thudding of my heart. It had seemed cold, very cold, during those moments, the cold of the tomb or of an infinite distance. Though it was a lovely voice—poor thing, poor thing! But I never saw her, saw nothing, only the blackness which gathers to itself all shadows. . . . And I never again called my dog Tita: my husband had been right for once. Now, if Nanina is lost, I can turn on the electric light and call boldly—I never miss that picture. . . . Later, I found the dog in the street outside."

Beyond the windows the animation of the evening was beginning. I heard the trains clanking and ringing, and the resonant strong voices of workmen returning home; and in the room, too, the sounds had regained their proportions. Nanina began to bark comfortably. No one was waiting: the story had expelled all shadows.

Lovers' Meeting

It was the ideal afternoon of a May day. Down below, ants moved along their tracks, and we flew over a model of Petworth, over miniature bare slopes, over towns and then over a marbled sea. The plane was crowded. A few "good-timers" were still there, faithful to an ideal that grew increasingly difficult to follow, loyal to their favourite beat; Paris for Whitsun.

"I may as well have a holiday," my neighbour remarked, a smooth-faced, rather handsome Jew of the Stock Exchanges. "I shall never have another. I join up next month."

In the enormous omnibus, dashing up from Le

Bourget, several fat women, rolling luxuriously at each turn of the road against their neighbours, made friends with them in this way. The men rolled back at them, hip to hip, with a *can-can*-like audacity: (the local atmosphere must have affected them). Though so near, the noise forced them to shout to one another.

"I always say there's no place like Paris!" they yelled. "You feel different directly you get here. . . . Especially now, with all the chestnuts in flower. It ought to be lovely. . . . And Josephine Baker is back at the old Casino! I *love* her, don't you?"

"Shan't we look silly if the Germans invade Holland and Belgium, and we can't get back? . . . But they won't: they can't: of course they won't, or our people wouldn't have let us come. . . . Yes it was quite easy. I was surprised. But I felt I wanted a change; growing stale in Brighton all those months. . . . Look, there's *Le Lapin Vert!* It's still open then? Someone said it was shut."

The next morning, Friday, I was woken at five by wailing sirens, and again at eight by the voice of the speaker on the French Radio, his calm and politeness exaggerated a thousandfold by the impersonality of the instrument. Moreover, the very loudness of its amplification made it sound as though the announcer were glad and the news were good. No one would dare to give bad tidings in such a tone. . . . The German armies had invaded Holland, Belgium and Luxemburg during the night, and had launched their great attack on the West.

It was difficult for me to know whether to continue my journey to Italy. I had been told not to go "if the situation deteriorated." At moments I thought that the dissolution of three further independent states marked such a stage. Besides, I knew that Italy was planning to enter the war, was convinced of it. Accordingly I cabled to the authorities, "Shall I still proceed Italy" . . . After three days of suspense, and of mingling with crowds walking up and down in the holiday sunshine, the reply came, on the very afternoon on which my train was due to leave.

"Think you had better continue but must be on your own responsibility."

I cabled back, "Proceeding Italy this afternoon but consider Tennysons celebrated lines theirs not to reason why theirs but to do or die would have lost in vigour had poet added further line on their own responsibility Sitwell," and drove to the Gare de Lyon.

The train happened to be the last permitted to reach Italy by the Simplon route. When we left, there was still some doubt as to whether the Swiss Government would allow it to enter Switzerland. But the conductors, who, looking in their hats and uniforms like overgrown telegraph-boys, stood poising pencils above charts, remained sanguine. It was impossible to divine their race, they belonged to the blue-chinned international tribes of the European *wagons-lits,* super gipsies with a languid *chic* all their own. They showed no animus. Nothing would happen: why should it? The Italians would not enter the war. . . . But Sanctions, those Sanctions!

As usual I reached the station too early, so having secured my compartment, I walked up and down the platform, watching fellow-passengers arrive; Balkan diplomats, with sleeked hair and high, giggling voices, returning home, French business men, Americans *en route* for their ships at Naples; and an enlarged—you could not have said *fat*—middle-aged Frenchwoman, much painted, with very golden hair and dark eyebrows and with several extensions of personality outside herself; jingling bangles provided, for example, music for every gesture, and there were cigarette cases and holders, bags in which to lose things and, finally, a minute, high-stepping griffon which, with a collar of bells, also contributed its own music for each step it took. A coat was strapped to its middle to keep it warm. (It was so small, the creature, that it made me think of Jean Cocteau's story of the woman who bought from a Paris dealer a little angel of a dog in a coat, with little shoes even on its feet. Naturally she was obliged to give a large sum for such a treasure, but none the less delighted with her purchase, brought it home. Once safely there, she left it for a few minutes alone in the drawing-room while she found it some food. . . . When she returned the little creature had run up the curtain; it was a rat, cleverly disguised and decked out.)

The owner of bangles and griffon was certainly very conspicuous. . . . Nevertheless the least conspicuous person on the platform was at the same time the most noticeable to myself, as she walked slowly up and down the platform. She was a woman of between sixty and seventy, bulky, dressed in black, with a puffy, emotional face, its flush emphasized, as is so often the case, by the whiteness of her hair. It was a kindly, silly face, and of a kind often encountered. She was, no doubt, a person who obeyed the conventions and who, while good in the sense of being generous and amiable, was also greedy and, to some mild extent, pleasure-loving, indulgent to herself as to others. She might have been the original of Miss Frances Cornford's

> Why do you walk in the fields with gloves,
> O fat, white woman whom nobody loves,
> Missing so much and so much?

Yes, somewhat self-indulgent. And she had the air of one who was used invariably to kindness, had always been protected. Yet her face held the attention: there was more in it than that; something mad and tragic, the dignity of Lear in his senseless, abnegatory abandon. Her blue-grey eyes, unimaginative and rather protruding, were strained and straining, full of emotion, did not see, but nevertheless saw, surely, beyond the objects at which she looked. Her mouth, which many years ago must have been so pretty, though its pouting had now, at her age, grown so ridiculous—worked the whole time as if she were talking. . . . One could not help wondering about her, because of the contrast between her appearance of being so ordinary, her mobile, puffy face, and the attitude and the mask of classic grief which her pose and countenance sometimes assumed. . . . But the passengers were getting in, the train was starting.

Next morning I sat in my *wagon-lit,* watching the touchingly beautiful Italian landscape roll by, under the tender early light. This country of mountain and lake pulled at the heart-strings, even if this were the first time you saw it; still more if you were familiar with trees and flowers, and loved the people as I did. But, under the lightness and sweetness of the air could be detected the stench of the treachery infecting it. Now we were passing Baveno, and Stresa, Isola Bella with its marble decks and pinnacles, and old trees in shrillest green leaf lay like full-rigged ships above the calm, mirror-like water. . . . How often had I seen it, how often had I done this journey! It seemed just the same. . . . Suddenly I heard a voice, hesitating and sad, speaking behind me, from the doorway in broken English.

There stood the old woman in black, her eyes seeming fuller and more brimming as the light from the windows fell direct on her puffy, discoloured face. Her whole attitude even through the jolting of the train, seemed inspired by some unbearable dignity, forced upon her in rigid, unwelcome mould, as though a great sculptor had chosen for once to shape a conception out of a medium so unsuitable as to make it all the more astonishing in its effect.

"Do you speak English?" she asked. "Forgive me, but I must talk to someone. I cannot stop talking. I am a bit crazy, I know. But I do not know what to do or what I should have done. I come from Belgium; you cannot believe what I have seen; my own son, home on leave, seized out of my own house before my eyes, by German soldiers, before I knew we were at war. I could not follow him. I do not know whether he is alive or dead. Perhaps I should have stayed there, but I did not know what to do, and all my friends were leaving? . . . And the roads, the refugees, the poor refugees; two days to go a few miles that in peace-time would take an hour. No pity, no pity anywhere. I saw Louvain burning for the second time. . . . I do not know; what could I do? Oh, what could I have done? I could not follow my son, they would not let me. My friends made me go to Paris, and from there, from the Embassy, I telephoned to my husband, whom I am joining—he is our Consul-General in Venice. All my life I have loved him, but now he is old, and when at last, we were able to get him on the telephone, he could not hear well. He could not understand about our son. He thought I should not have left him there— but what could I do? They seized him and took him away. And I never stop thinking of him, saying to myself, what could I do or have done? . . . The poor refugees, struggling, running down the roads, all of them the colour of dust, and some lying where they fell in the ditch, not troubling to get up. . . . You don't mind my talking. I must talk to someone, or I shall go mad. (But I am a little mad already, I know.) . . . I could not have believed what I have seen. All my life I have been *dévote,* but now I ask *Le Bon Dieu* how He could have permitted it? The fires, the people, the poor people, running. . . ."

There was a pause. The sweet, calm Italian country sped past the windows. In the corridor, just outside, the fussy, spindle-legged, *petit-maître* griffon danced and pranced and sneezed and thrilled with pleasure, his bells jingling at each movement and curvet, while his mistress sounded her bangles, giggled in the manner she had for more than a generation found attractive, and shouted, slapping the front of her thigh with a fat hand, "Ninon, Ninon chéri, viens voir Maman." The dog danced more than ever, its eyes bulging with pleasure.

The monologue in the doorway started again. "All in three days! The roads choked, and I saw the faces of the German airmen as they dived and machine-gunned us, saw them laughing. . . . No pity anywhere in the world. . . . And my son! . . . What am I to say to my husband? He will be at the station. He is perhaps angry and I do not know how to explain, do not know what to say . . ."

The Glow-Worm

When the war broke out in 1939, Sebastian Corble—*of course* you know the name—was nearly
forty. At first sight he still kept a look of youth, almost
of being boyish; except that he seemed too large, just
as a child-impersonator on the stage often succeeds in
giving an impression of being childish, but in an over-
life-size manner. His hair, though a little thinner than
in Oxford days, still retained a thick golden gloss as, in
rather tattered array, aureole-like, it encircled his round
cranium. Each individual hair, each tooth, each pore,
seemed to claim more value in the whole presentation
of his appearance than formerly; that was all. He was
pale, and this lack of colour imparted to him, if the

light came strong enough and from the right direction, a certain aspect of nobility, an air, almost, of that holy illumination to be found in the transparent countenances of the boyish saints depicted in late nineteenth-century church windows: but from this lack of humanity, his charm—his all-pervading, rather rancid charm—rescued him.

In every succeeding generation, a journalist makes a substantial fortune out of certain subjects; gardens, fashionable chit-chat, spiritualism; but who would ever have imagined that in a wicked age—for, to the good people of to-day it seems as though any age in which the world was not dedicated to the high mission of destruction and massacre must have been a wicked age, lacking in democratic ideals—a fortune could have been made by the skilful exploitation of mere goodness and domesticity? This, then, had been Sebastian's discovery. To him it had been left to find out and explain that religion could be "fun," and eternity, "cosy." He could make his million readers feel at home in Heaven. A more masculine Mrs. Beeton, he would sometimes begin an article by describing the "divine" new curtains in his bedroom, and end with an account of his child, Little Tessa, talking to him of God. But he did not belong to the Mrs. Winniver School, he could be strong as well as good. Strength, rather than sour whimsy, tempered so much sweetness, and he was so adept at scenting-out and denouncing moral dangers. Such authors as D. H. Lawrence and James Joyce he had flogged through his daily, and flayed in his weekly, columns. The peroration of his famous Sunday article denouncing Joyce's *Ulysses* is still remembered by many who have never read the book: "And after that I had climbed a little hill to gaze in the eyes of God's Primroses, I rested, but still the foul miasma of that book pursued me, until I cried aloud, 'Psah! Who will sweeten my nostrils with an ounce of civet?' ... And a small sweet voice behind me said, 'I will, Daddy!' ... And there behind me, in the sunshine of that spring day, stood little Tessa. Rather would I that she quaffed the hemlock cup than that one day she should read another such book, if another such book there should be!"

Yet, sweetness always followed such outbursts of strength, and, on Sundays especially, a great army of admirers turned to him for comfort; and oh, the comfort, pressed down and of full measure, which they received! Round them he distilled the sweetness of his own home. Of difficult domestic material, even,—of his wife's telling him not to be silly or of Tessa having German measles—he was able to make some of his most appealing articles. He was never ashamed of sentimentality, and when a reader read one word, he knew what the next would be. To give an instance, in no way remarkable, I recall a "splash" headline of

Open the Door!

"Wot's Wong? by Sebastian Corble"; a description of how Little Tessa tottered up to him on her "baby feet," and, "gazing up into his eyes," "hissed out"—no, I am not giving you the right counter, I mean "lisped pleadingly"—"Daddy, wot's wong?" while a linnet flew in at the window, and trilled its way backward and forward over their heads as if in an effort to comfort them.

And something *was* wrong: for, good in the main as Sebastian found both this world and the next, a sense of discouragement, an inevitable feeling of disappointment, would sometimes assail him. For example, his fellow writers were often inappreciative, seemed to perceive the beauty of his writing no more than the peculiar virtue of his life. Again, Margaret, his wife whom he really adored, was too retiring, threatening to leave him if he brought her into an article. She would not play any of the parts he would have liked to assign to her, while Little Tessa, to be frank, trod the boards too heavily. . . . But then Tessa, everybody said, was "just like her father."

Thus both father and daughter lived, you might almost say battled, for publicity. She had become nearly as popular as he was, yet he dared not stop it, for in a sense they were complementary and, also, there were the funds she brought in to be considered. Her vogue was, all the same, fantastic. Every autumn, a calendar, specially illustrated, was on sale for the new year; reluctantly, no doubt, edited and selected by her father, it contained a gem, in the form of a question, for every day in the week: Jan: 1. "Why is the snow white, Daddy?" Jan: 2. "Why did God choose white, Daddy?" Jan: 3. "Is it because white is good, Daddy?" and so on, seasonally, until the end of the year. . . . Admiration grew, sales mounted. Her adherents founded "The Tiny Tessa Tub" (she could not say "Club," her father had written) and thousands of children who modelled themselves on her, wore a special button, with a photograph of her enamelled upon it, in the buttonholes of their coats.

Soon she would be six. . . . "Nasty little publicity-hound," her father reflected to himself in an access of irritation, it was really time for her to give up all that baby-business, and be content to merge decorously into his background. But such, plainly, was not her intention. . . . And she was as clever as she was good. Often she sent for representatives of the press on her own initiative (already she could use the telephone as well as if she were twenty!); and if he were to become too repressive, she was quite capable of summoning interviewers, and with those great, welling eyes of hers, of blurting out to them, "You don't think my Daddy's jealous! It's a wicked 'fought'." (That would be a nice sentiment to have to record on the calendar for 1939.)

Open the Door!

. . . Of course, he was devoted to the little thing (he must be, he knew): but sometimes he wondered in his heart whether he really cared much for children. His wife would say, "Don't be irritable with her, Basty; she is too much *like you,* that's all it is." And then, in her turn, she would warn the little girl, "Now Tessa! I've told you. Don't irritate Daddy on purpose. . . . And I've said before, you're too young to be photographed for the *Daily Mirror!* And don't whine!"

He knew that, for all his goodness, he *was* irritable. The strain of writing, the strain of money-making, the strain of always being good, in time had caused him to be afflicted with insomnia. His own goodness, as it were, kept him awake at night. He found it difficult to endure the ridicule of the music-halls, as well as that of the comic papers—for, in addition to being a very popular writer, his renowned virtue had made him a very popular joke; a combination that could only exist in this country. But he did not allow such mockery to deflect him from the straight and narrow path. Virtue still offered him a very glittering reward. Think of those articles, those great articles that rolled away into infinity! Even the titles of some of them come back to me, "I Believe in the Old Stories," "Saints Have Halos," "Don't Insure Your Life, Insure for After-Life!" "Cleanse the Stables!" "Who's Who in Heaven." Politicians praised him and sought his advice: but somehow, his popularity survived their fleeting shadows. The immense esteem in which he was held extended its bounds to the United States, the citizens of which adopted the new cult with fury. Tessa, too, remained more than a good second. . . . It was gratifying. . . . Yet, as he would have phrased it, The maggot bitterness still dwelt in the heart of the rose. For people—some poor, lost, unregenerate and ungenerous souls—laughed at him in a disagreeable way: he knew it. In a news-film, for example, he had been shown making a speech at the opening of "The Tiny Tessa Garden of Friendship" on the roof of one of the great London stores, and the public had laughed till the words were inaudible.

Then war came—and with it that great advance of moral values everywhere in Great Britain that war is always said to bring us. The values of peacetime were precisely reversed. The Common Man, recognized as arbiter, now in his generosity did not denounce the political leaders and incompetent club-room soldiers who had betrayed the men and women of two generations, but instead turned fiercely on the artists and writers of the last twenty years who had given that period its chief claim to distinction. Anything that helped us to kill, was good, and Sebastian's goodness helped the killing, and so was better. His former popularity became an all-devouring rage. And many writers in the press openly gave expression to an opinion that countless readers echoed; "If only we could have Sebastian Corble or Our Gracie as Prime Minister, the War would soon be over!"

He worked day and night. The Government, observing his vast influence with public opinion, allowed him special facilities for directing it. . . . Scarcely ever was he at home in Hampstead now. One night he would spend in the Maginot Line ("impregnable as the front line of Heaven," he wrote), the second flying over the lines, the third on board a submarine, the fourth on a tank, the fifth on a destroyer in the North Sea, the sixth in the "Clipper" *en route* for a week's lecture in the United States. He was sent on picnics with soldiers and sailors and airmen and munition workers, he was allowed to attend Holy Service in the Desert during the Libyan War, he flew to Malta and back to collect money for Spitfires. He and War Publicity illumined each other equally. But, though the aid he rendered was invaluable, he wore himself to a shadow, spent himself utterly in the cause. Fortunately, the good, the real good, he was doing, gave him new strength (and think of the money he was earning, even if half of it went to the making of the war which was making him!). "You're a Saint," people used to say to him, and he was able to feel that there was a grain of truth in their praise.

There *was* something saintly about him now, and

the look of a saint, which he had always a little possessed, had greatly developed. And he was much less irritable and nervous, though he missed dreadfully his home. . . . At last, tired out but happy, in September 1940—just a few days before the first intensive bombing of London began—he went home for a week of rest, a week of utter peace.

Tessa looked forward to his home-coming even more than Margaret, for, with the coming of the war, she had swung a little into the background. She was nearly eight now, and had been very excited ever since she had heard the news. She smelt publicity again, her mother thought. It was so bad for her—and she prevented the child from telephoning to editors, to tell them that "Daddy was on his way home," or, as she put it to her mother, "to give them the low-down." . . . She was allowed to stay up for dinner, an unusual treat, the night he arrived.

Everyone had always noticed how very observant Tessa was. "So wonderful of a little thing like that to see everything," her parents' friends used to remark, with a secret sense of unease, and would then add, with a conscious and shameful lack of frankness, "But for all that, she's a thorough child; dear Little Tessa!" . . . After being fairly quiet throughout the meal until she had finally consumed the sweet, an ice-cream of which she was over-fond, she then proceeded to bounce up and down on her chair, on a new method she had discovered, until the room shook. Sebastian expelled all feelings of irritation and radiated love toward her; also on a new method he had discovered. He comforted himself, moreover, with the reflection that, if *he* were to dance about like that immediately after dinner, he would feel sick, very sick—but that was being uncharitable, he must be ever on the watch. "T*e*s-s*a* d*a*r-ling!" he called lovingly to her, dwelling on each syllable. . . . For a few moments she sat in silence, motionless, watching him—with suspicion, you might have thought, as if she imagined he was trying to gain some advantage over her—and then her restraint broke down, and suddenly, angrily, she burst out with:

"Daddy, what's that funny light round your forehead?"

For a moment her father's mood changed. "Silly little beast!" he reflected uncharitably, in a spasm of annoyance, "indulging in stupid fancies!" He said nothing, however: but, as the words passed through his mind, Tessa added, in a voice that showed traces of relief:

"It's gone now, Daddy!"

Margaret regarded the child with curiosity. It was evident to her that the child *had* seen something, which herself had missed.

"I didn't see anything, Tessa," she said. "What do you mean?"

The Glow-Worm

But Tessa jumped down from her chair and ran up to the nursery without answering. When her mother later went to say good-night, she found the child looking earnestly at her own head in the mirror.

The next day, Sebastian was busy. It was a Friday, and he had sent off an article to the *Sunday Debacle*. It was one of the best, literally the *best,* he had ever written. But all the time, even while composing it, Tessa's strange remark had hovered in his consciousness, behind every word and every thought. Probably the child had meant nothing; but it was odd. . . . And an unusual sense of contentment, of being at one with Nature and the Universe, seized upon him; a feeling of inner peace and satisfaction, as though he had been engaged in the utter fulfilment, physical as well as spiritual, not so much after the manner of a great painter executing a great picture, as of a peacock expanding its scintillant and jewelled tail, or a swan exchanging the ruffled beige of cygnetcy for its adult and undying white.

After tea, Tessa continued to eye him at intervals with a singular persistence: until her mother, misinterpreting the effect upon Sebastian (for this evening her intent gaze in no way troubled him), sent her to bed. She protested, but it was long past bedtime already, and she had only been allowed down to dinner last night on her solemn promise not to expect such a treat again. So she was led upstairs, moaning "But I want to see Daddy when it's dark."

Margaret and Sebastian went to bed early too that night, and in his prayers he made a special recommendation for notice and mercy on behalf of his "darling child, Little Tessa."

When they were called the following morning, the sunshine seemed to fall with peculiar strength upon the pillows. Before long, Margaret had to ask Sebastian to pull the blind down, so that the light did not catch her full in the eyes. Then they had breakfast in bed, and though himself did not so much notice the brightness of which she several times complained, somehow he could not succeed in arranging the blind to suit her. As soon as he had jumped out of bed, she would—almost before he had reached the window—cry, "That's better!", but the moment he got back into bed, she would declare that the light was dazzling her again. . . . A year ago, all this jumping in and out of bed at a woman's caprice would have irritated him; but not so now. He was master of himself. . . . He opened a letter. It proved to be from an admirer, and began, "You're a Saint, a *real* Saint!" . . . At this moment a suspicion, bordering upon a certainty, of the immense and impossible truth entered his brain.

It grew dark about eight o'clock that evening and, before dinner, he had a bath and changed. And it was

The Glow-Worm

while he was brushing his hair, in the dusk, in front of a looking-glass, that he first noticed the faint, bluish white radiance spreading after the fashion of a diadem or crown about his forehead. . . . He recognized it at once; a halo, it *was* a halo, plain, without the red bars to it one sometimes sees in church windows. (He was glad of that, he did not wish to be ostentatious.) His spontaneous feelings were those of gratification rather than of surprise, together—and this was odd—with a wish to hide this new spiritual distinction from his wife. . . . No, he had to admit it, he did *not* want her to see it—at any rate, not yet! So he had better avoid Tessa, who would be sure to spot it at once. . . . Otherwise, he was pleased. After all, it constituted an award from the highest authority. And it would aid his popularity and circulation. (In his mind's eye, he could already see the enormous placards round the tops of the buses, "Corble, The Man With Halo Writes For The 'Daily Dustbin' Only.")

At dinner, he turned up all the lights in the room so that his new nimbus should not be observed. Tessa was upstairs—he felt too tired, he said, to climb to say good-night to her—and Margaret noticed nothing unusual about him. The evening passed quietly and pleasantly enough, and they went to bed early. . . . Almost before Margaret's head touched the pillow she fell asleep. But Sebastian, on the other hand, found it unusually difficult to relax. The light from his head kept getting into his eyes. Even if he shut them, he could still perceive the glow. Really, it was blinding now! And the more patient he grew, the more careful not to become flustered or angry at this unnecessary waste of candlepower, and of the time he so urgently needed for repose, the stronger grew his aureole in intensity, a positive dazzle. . . . What a blessing, he reflected, that Margaret could not see it—and then, all at once, as he experienced a contradictory spasm of annoyance because she had not beheld, or *would* not behold, it, a wilful manifestation of a sort of spiritual blindness that afflicted her—the light faded a little of itself, and slumber in consequence engulfed him.

Though he was on holiday he devoted the next morning, Saturday, to seeing his publishers and to good works. He lunched at his club, and then visited old friends in the East End, insisting on reading to them his favourite extracts from *Stories of Venice,* and from a new book by the head of the Foreign Office, entitled *The Trail of the Hun.* He wound up with "a few little things of my own." He did not return home until after dark (they were going to have supper late that night). And, as he walked home from the tube station, once or twice he heard an angry, brusque voice calling from the darkness, "Keep that light down, man, can't you?" or "Don't flash it about like that, or you'll find yourself somewhere you don't expect. Didn't you hear the sirens?"

Tessa was already in bed and her father again alleged that he was too tired to go upstairs and say good-night to her. She was anxious to see him, it appeared. And Margaret pleaded for her:

"After all, Basty," she said, "the child is devoted to you. You know she is, and you oughtn't to neglect her."

But he would not give way. The doctors had told him not to exert himself or do anything that was against his inclinations.

Still Margaret noticed no change in him, and they enjoyed a quiet evening until they had just finished supper, when the bombs of the first great night attack began to rain down on London. He must write about it at once for the New York paper. ("Hot News from Sebastian Corble," he could see it already splashed across the page.) What did danger matter, after all, he asked himself, and slipped into the garden, alone, for Margaret preferred to stop indoors. He repressed his annoyance as he tumbled over a stone toadstool with a tin gnome sitting on it, and had soon reached the little terrace at the end. Once there, he forgot everything else in the interest and horror of the scene below.

About a quarter of an hour later, the telephone bell rang in the house. Margaret answered it. A voice said,

Open the Door!

"Is that you, Mrs. Corble? This is North Hampstead Police Station. We are informed that someone is signalling from your garden, but we know you too well to suppose that you would permit any foreigners about the place. You don't think, perhaps, as Miss Tessa as got hout and is being mischeavious with a light?"

Margaret promised to make inquiries, and then to speak to them again in a few minutes' time. But, no sooner had she put the receiver down, than she heard an urgent knocking at the door. She opened it, and a very angry and official air-raid warden informed her that he had seen lights floating in the garden.

"There's too much of that sort of thing going on," he added. "Shooting's too good for 'em."

She contrived to calm the new-comer by telling him that she had already promised to investigate the matter for the police, and that her husband, Sebastian Corble, was there, and together they would search the place thoroughly.

"Oh, I didn't know it was Mrs. *Sebastian* Corble to whom I have the honour of speaking," the warden answered. "I'm a great admirer of your husband's. There's real *goodness* for you, and *guts* too," and left, mollified.

Sebastian's virtue had its uses, his wife thought, as she shut the door, but, all the same, life was growing

294

insupportable with all these silly scares. Was it likely that anyone could get into the garden and signal? . . . But she had better tell Sebastian, so she went out to join him. . . . It was certainly mysterious that *two* complaints should have been received. What *could* be the explanation, just hysteria, she wondered? . . . Then, as her eyes grew accustomed to the darkness, she understood! Sebastian's halo was visible, its pale yet scintillant radiation coming and going like that of a firefly.

But the effect of it upon her was indeed unexpected. Perhaps the noise of the bombing had made her nervous to-night, though she had not been aware of it, for she laughed out loud, and could not stop, laughed all the more as, when this ribald sound asserted itself beneath all the banging from earth and sky, she watched the aureole of her husband's sainthood and suffering glow yet more brightly.

Weakly, nearly crying, she said to him, "Basty, *please* go inside, or you'll be fined!" . . . With a gentle air of reproach and dignity, he asked her why she laughed, and she told him that the police and the A.R.P. authorities thought they had caught a foreign spy signalling from the garden. "And now," she added, "I must go inside too, and tell them what I've found. 'It's only my husband's new halo, Inspector.'"

Neither of them slept well that night. In the morning he said to her apologetically:

"Darling, I'm afraid all that dreadful bombing kept you awake last night?"

"No, Sebastian," she answered, "I didn't mind the noise, but your halo kept getting in my eyes. I can't share my bed with a Saint; that's all there is to it!"

They had a quarrel about this—both of them were feeling rather on edge no doubt—and his radiance temporarily faded.

He looked in the glass before leaving the house, and decided that in the daytime it only slightly accentuated his usual pallor, and a certain distinction which he hoped he had always possessed. Of course, if he put his head back on a cushion, for instance, the light played upon it, but that merely resembled the "shaft of sunlight," which, in a romantic novel, always falls upon the hero's face as he is saying good-bye. . . . No, it was in the evenings that it was a nuisance.

He did not talk much to Margaret, for he wrote all day in his room, and only saw her at luncheon, when she was engaged in keeping Tessa's mind occupied. At seven, he had to addresss a meeting of the Golders Green Branch of the Tiny Tessa Tub. . . . Usually he walked about bare-headed, but to-night, without Margaret seeing him do it—for he did not wish to provoke another of those very trying hysterical scenes, they must be so bad for her—he encircled his head with the two

regulation thicknesses of tissue-paper. That should prevent his being stopped, or threatened with a summons,
people would just imagine that his cap was too big
for him, and he was trying to make it fit. . . . In
the brightly lighted hall nothing would show. . . . So
he could take the whole thing off in the cloak-room
and leave it there until after the meeting.

Alas, on the return journey, after the meeting, he
found that his attempts to comply with the regulations
had been of no avail. Men could not understand. For
them, a halo was merely a reprehensible light, to be
treated with hard words and fury. The old complaints
sounded from the darkness. "Switch it out man, can't
you?" "I'll summon yer for this, young feller, if yer
don't alter yer wise. I'll tike yer nime and address,"
"Wot yer think yer doing? A blarsted light'ouse, are
yer?" . . . And, which made the scene more distressing,
at each undeserved rebuke, the light of its own accord
grew stronger.

No peace anywhere! But one must be good and
meek and gentle. He took off his coat in the darkness
and covered his head with it. Thus he managed to
reach home without being arrested.

He could not, when he arrived, avoid going to say
good-night to Tessa, for, as well as its being Sunday,
they were sending her away to-morrow to avoid the

bombing. . . . She had been unusually reserved the whole day, but now she threw her arms round her father and said simply, sleepily:

"Good-night, Daddy, I'm a glow-worm too!"

Her father looked at her, but she must have fancied herself into the statement. It would be most unfair if the daughter—even of such a father—were to receive the same award. He could see no sign of it, not a ray.

That night, alone, in the spare bedroom, he thought things out. . . . A Saint has no place for earthly ties, he decided. Like Saints of Old—was it St. Andrew in the hymn?—he must leave home and kindred. He made no charges, no allegations of want of faith, never even reproached Margaret, but the next morning he left to join the Fleet and gather material for a new and stirring article. He arrived just in time for the famous Battle of the Bombs, as the press called it,—the only journalist present. It was the first scoop of the Saint. But the Admiral never discovered that it was the trail of a halo that, by indicating the position of the ships, was responsible for so much damage. In whatever direction Sebastian moved, it was sure to be followed by an explosion and a cry, "By Jove, that was a narrrow squeak!"

Always, he was in the thick of things. Even if he went on a lecture tour, every town at which he stopped the night would be raided, and this, in turn, would provide him with the material for a splendid and heartening article the next day. (To protect himself against the police, he had now adopted a steel helmet with a special lining of cotton-wool. It appeared to be impervious. But often, when he was sure of being alone, its weight would induce him to take it off for a moment.) His rhetoric was unmatched, and he became the highest paid journalist in the country. Little Tessa was hopelessly outclassed.

"He can't always escape like that," people used to say as they read him, "One day the enemy will bag him!" But they never did. For, in the end, peace came, and with it the great deterioration of moral values which is always said to manifest itself in a period when killing again becomes a sin. In time—in a very, very short time—the public changed its allegiance and went whoring after new gods. The Common Man—still, of course, arbiter of taste—no longer read Sebastian Corble's strong stuff on the evils of peace, but threw him, together with Shakespeare, on the scrap-heap, and turned with relief to the life stories of the new Hollywood favourites. Before long, a bitter note crept into Sebastian's denunciations: they grew still more strong, and, in these degenerate days of which I write, as they grew stronger, the readers became fewer. And, as the note of bitterness deepened, so did the radiance fade, until Sebastian Corble was mere man again.